I0518921

Roaming the Fringe

A Collection of Short Stories

Michael Beauchamp

Eleusis Press

Roaming the Fringe

Copyright © 2016 by Michael Beauchamp

Published by Eleusis Press

2009 North 7th Street, Phoenix, Arizona, 85006

eleusisimages@gmail.com

Printed and bound in the United States of America

For Karen

Table of Contents

Keeper of the Cubes

He was known as the Keeper of the Cubes. In reality, his name was Ron. He was little more than a custodian, but this fact does not diminish the importance of his work. Ron's role was vital and he took his job very seriously. The continued existence of the human species, in its new and ostensibly evolved state, depended on *him*.

Ron was a simple and happy man. He performed his duties cheerfully and never complained. The truth is, no one was around to *hear* his complaints. You see, Ron was the last of the Organics – the very last soul who still occupied a human body. The other survivors had recently migrated to their Cubes. Their minds now existed eternally in highly advanced and totally convincing computer simulations. Each Cube was a distinct and custom-created universe, tailor-made for the individual and designed to provide maximum joy and pleasure. You might wonder why I refer to people as *survivors*. Settle in and I'll tell you the story.

The exodus from three-dimensional reality was preceded by an almost equally momentous event – an event that would drastically reduce the number of people who would make the transition. The majority of the Earth's population never knew what was coming. They were totally unaware of the plans being made in secret to escape the upcoming global cataclysm.

The ELE – or Extinction Level Event – had been predicted many years in advance of its arrival. The data was strong, the projections irrefutable. The outcome was inevitable. Scientists all over the world tracked the massive asteroid as it raced toward the planet on its trajectory of death. Decisions of grave consequence were made. Not long after it was realized that the event could not be prevented, it was decided that the general public must never know. What good would it serve the average man and woman to be aware of their imminent doom?

Somewhere, somehow, someone who called the shots initiated a highly classified project. The brightest minds of the time were called into action and given a mission: find a way to save at least a small portion of the race. It was a huge undertaking of profound significance. Those who worked on the project were prepared to do whatever it would take to succeed, using all available resources, including cutting-edge, experimental technology. It was a multinational effort. With the threat of total annihilation of the species looming, the world's political, regional, ideological, and racial divisions were quickly forgotten.

Scientists, engineers, physicians, and computer programmers worked in deep underground military facilities, closely monitored by military personnel. The underground bases had been there for many years prior, but were expanded and connected into a vast network that crisscrossed the planet. Eventually, the project would be confined to one large cavern – Ron's domain – but in the early years, the operation involved hundreds of hollowed-out rooms and thousands of individuals.

Countless options were considered. Innumerable theories were explored. The breakthrough came in the field of computer science and the development of neural mapping. It was discovered that a complete digital reproduction of the brain, including the thoughts and memories contained within it, could be saved and inserted into a machine running a simulation program. This effectively rendered a flesh and blood body obsolete. This was convenient, since it was thought that the Earth – the surface, at least – would be uninhabitable for many centuries after the ELE.

The machine that ran the simulation was a small box that could fit in the palm of one's hand. These boxes came to be known as Cubes. All of the survivors could, once uploaded to their individual Cubes, be stacked in one room, where they would exist in the eternal bliss of their choosing. This made any future attempts to repopulate the Earth unnecessary, the project leaders reasoned. To them, living in a digital simulation as an immortal mind was the next logical step in human evolution. And so, even before the asteroid struck the planet, the migration began. Each chosen survivor underwent the process of neural mapping and insertion into his or her custom Cube. Each survivor entered a unique, self-contained reality.

A volunteer had been chosen to remain behind to ensure that the last participant in the project made the transition successfully. The volunteer was Ron, who had been working as a janitor in the main facility since the inception of the project. He was an average man of average intellect who was well-liked by all who knew him. He had a calm, pleasant demeanor that made those around him feel good, despite the serious implications of their work.

Ron's task was simple: once the last person had been scanned and was ready for insertion, Ron simply had to push a key to complete the transfer. Once that was done, Ron was to have free reign of the entire facility and complete use of its stocks and amenities for as long as he lived. This suited him fine, for he was a solitary man by nature. He would also have the company of his best friend, Bruno the Cat. As part of his normal duties as janitor, Ron was asked to keep the Cube Room tidy while he was alive and able. Someone once referred to him as the Keeper of the Cubes and the name stuck.

Deep below the surface of the Earth, the time came

for the last upload. A man lay on a gurney, his head covered in sensors. He was wired up and scanned. Ron pressed a key on the control panel and the man's consciousness lingered in limbo for a few moments as his mind was inserted into his Cube. When the upload was complete, Ron removed the sensors and wheeled the body into a vault with all the others. This did not disturb him, for he knew that the man wasn't *really* dead. Having completed his work, Ron returned to his quarters, whistling as he walked through the deserted, cavernous tunnels.

Many months went by. Ron lived a quiet, solitary life, completely incognizant of what was happening on the surface. He was quite content to be alone in the massive facility. He spent his days reading books, watching old movies, snacking on the ample rations in the storerooms, and wandering the extensive tunnel system, often with Bruno trotting happily beside him. Ron did not need a Cube. For him, life was already perfect.

Everything changed for Ron on the day he discovered the monitoring room. He stumbled upon it accidentally while exploring an area of the facility that had previously been off-limits. It seemed like a chance discovery at the time, but in retrospect, considering the subsequent events, it could be said that the hand of providence had guided him.

The door was unlocked. Ron turned the knob and opened it, expecting to find a dorm room or perhaps a utility closet. What he saw startled him. It was, in appearance, a control center or command bunker. The immense room was full of computer equipment and desks. All four walls were covered in high-resolution video screens that were segmented into small squares, each displaying a different image. In awe, Ron stepped into the room. Bruno the Cat followed close behind.

"Gee, Bruno," Ron said, "looks like someone forgot

to turn off the TVs!"

Ron couldn't believe his eyes. It was like watching a thousand movies playing at once. He scanned the room, marveling at the technological sophistication, delighting in the bountiful entertainment the room would no doubt provide. His delight rapidly transformed into extreme unease when he realized that each and every screen seemed to be displaying a scene of violence and horror.

"I don't like scary movies," Ron said quietly.

What was being shown on the screens was more than scary – the scenes were truly disturbing. In one scene, a man was being tortured with jagged, rusty metal implements by figures in black cloaks. In another, a terrified woman was being chased through a forest by a lumbering, menacing creature. Swarms of spiders, pools of blood, drownings, monsters, fire, and pain – Ron's mind reeled at the nightmarish images. He watched as people fell from buildings, dangled from cliffs, went mad at the sight of grotesque and obscene things, and grappled with dark, spectral entities. It was like peering into a thousand hells. It was then that he noticed something even more unsettling – he *recognized* some of the individuals on the screens. They were project members, his co-workers and friends.

"These aren't movies," Ron said. "I know these people."

It was a shocking realization. The characters were not actors and it was obvious to Ron that the people were in real distress. The epiphany struck – Ron was seeing what was happening in the Cubes. Far from existing in an eternal paradise, the Cube dwellers were being tormented and they were suffering. Something had gone dreadfully wrong.

"I have to help them, Bruno."

Ron was the only one who *could* help. He was the only one left in the facility – the only one who was even *aware* that a thousand minds were trapped in a thousand virtual hells. For those who were completely immersed in the simulations, Ron knew the suffering would be far from virtual – the agony and horror they were experiencing would be very real. It was useless for Ron to speculate on what had gone wrong. All he knew – and needed to know – was that the Cubes were manifesting the subconscious fears of the users instead of their desires.

"They don't even know it isn't real. They forgot where they came from and who they are."

Ron's heart ached in empathy for the trapped souls. He was a simple janitor and did not know how to even begin to help them. His first thought was to destroy the Cubes, but he knew that it would destroy the minds contained within them as well. This was not something he could bring himself to do. He wondered how hard it would be to reverse the process. Could he somehow reinsert their consciousnesses back into their bodies? The bodies were being kept in a freezer vault. Would they still be viable vessels? Even if they were, Ron still had no idea how to operate the equipment or program the computers. He had been trained to do a very simple task on top of his regular custodial duties – push a button and wheel a gurney.

"If only I could reach them somehow," Ron mused. "If only I could get them to remember and realize what is happening."

Ron began to explore the control room. He went from desk to desk and panel to panel, examining the complex equipment. Bruno the Cat followed him faithfully. Ron found a myriad of keypads, switches, dials, and buttons. Most of the technology was beyond his ability to comprehend. It was all so overwhelming. He began to feel discouraged and dismayed... then he saw something that gave him hope and sparked an idea. Mounted on a desk in the middle of the room was a microphone on an adjustable stand.

"Well, now," Ron said as he sat down at the desk. "Could this be what I think it is?"

Ron pulled the microphone toward him and tapped on it instinctively. Nothing happened. He studied the control panel in front of him. He spotted a switch at the base of the stand that said ON/OFF, below which was a numbered keypad. Along with the numbers 0 through 9, the keypad had two additional keys labeled CHANNEL SELECT and ALL CHANNELS.

"Interesting," Ron said. "Very interesting. What do you think, Bruno? Do you think this will let us talk to the Cubes? No way to know unless we try, right?"

Bruno did not respond. The cat curled up at Ron's feet and settled in for a nap.

"Even if this works, what should I say? I'm a little nervous. I don't want to scare anybody anymore than they already are."

Ron took a few minutes to gather his thoughts. It didn't help much. He decided to simply improvise. He reached over and pressed the ALL CHANNELS button before switching the microphone on.

"Uh, hello," Ron stammered into the microphone. "Can anyone hear me?"

Ron looked up at the monitors in front of him. There was so much going on in so many scenes, it was hard to tell if he had been heard. He paused before trying again.

"My name is Ron. I'm the custodian. I think there's been a malfunction. I think there's something wrong with the Cubes. Can anybody hear me? I want to help you."

On one of the screens, Ron noticed a woman who was apparently trying to escape from a dingy concrete room. She suddenly ceased her panicked search for a way out and looked up at the ceiling. Though he could not hear what she was saying, Ron could read her lips as she cried out, "Yes! I can hear you! Please... *help* me!"

Ron was astonished. He was momentarily at a loss for words and too stunned to continue. He then noticed that many others had also apparently heard him. They were looking up and around in all directions trying to locate the source of the mysterious voice – *Ron's* voice, which came to them like the voice of God in their darkest hour. Some people began to cry. Some were frozen in fear. A few even dropped to their knees and began to pray. Ron grasped the microphone, took a deep breath, and spoke again.

"Okay, good. You can hear me. Please, don't be afraid. What you are experiencing isn't real. It's an experiment that went wrong. I need you to try and remember where you came from. I need you to try and recall who you once were."

Nascent awareness dawned on the faces of a small number of Cube dwellers. Ron could see them beginning to understand. Still, Ron could see confusion and fear reigning in the minds of most of them.

"You are living in a simulation, a virtual reality contained within a Cube," Ron continued. "It was supposed to be an eternal paradise, but something went wrong. To me, it looks like the program has tapped into your deepest fears. Instead of a perfect dream world, you are creating your own nightmares. None of it is real, though."

A bright flash of light on a screen to his right caught Ron's attention. He looked over in time to see an extraordinary sight – a man was standing in a jungle surrounded by lions, but everything in the scene was frozen. The freeze had happened while two male lions were moving in for the kill. They were suspended in the air, claws mere feet from the man's head. The man had his hands up and his eyes closed. He opened his eyes now and looked around as the lions remained frozen in midair. A smile appeared on the man's face.

Ron watched in amazement as the screen flashed with a bright, white light once again and the scene changed. The man was no longer in the jungle – he was now reclining in a chair on a gorgeous, tropical island beach with white sand, gentle waves on the clear, blue water, bright sun and swaying palm trees – the man had created for himself a scene of idyllic beauty and serenity.

"You can change it!" Ron cried into the microphone. "It's true! I've seen it happen. It can happen for *you*... for *all* of you! Concentrate, focus, *believe*."

Ron continued to survey the video walls and saw it happen for more and more of the Cube dwellers. He began to cry tears of joy as he watched scene after scene transform. Horrific, violent, terrifying realities became worlds of joy and bliss. It was, for lack of a better word, miraculous.

For the rest of the day and through the night, Ron sat in his chair transfixed by the transmutations occurring all around him. One by one, the scenes in each Cube became depictions of paradise. Ron was incredibly relieved and deeply satisfied that he had been able to help the Cube dwellers, but he knew, in his heart, that he could not take total credit. It was they, and their forces of will and powers of belief, that had done the true work.

"You know, Bruno, I wonder if even regular guys like me couldn't do something similar in our so-called *real* lives?"

For the first time since he had entered the underground facility, Ron's thoughts turned to what might be happening on the surface. He had a sudden yearning to be outside and, even more unusual for him, he had a sudden yearning to be in the company of others.

"Feel like going on an adventure, Bruno? It might be a good idea to check out what's going on up top. Maybe things aren't as bad as they said they would be. There might even be other *people* out there! We should go and take a look, don't you think?"

Ron got up and nudged Bruno the Cat, who woke up, yawned, and stretched luxuriously. Ron led the cat out of the control room and walked down the wide corridor toward the elevator that would take them to the surface. It was now morning, an abstract concept in the depths of the facility. Ron smiled as he imagined what it would be like to feel sunlight on his face once again.

Peter and the Satellite

We all have bad days. Some days make you wish that you
hadn't gotten out of bed that morning. Some days make you
wonder if it would have been better if you had never been
born at all. Some days make you feel like your life is one big
cosmic joke, perpetrated on you by a sadistic, malevolent
universe that delights in your suffering and is intent on
driving you totally, irrevocably insane, purely for its own
amusement. That is the kind of day that Peter was having. To
be fair, it actually started the night before.

Peter lives alone. Peter is a slob. Peter likes to eat
greasy fast food with his bare hands directly out of a
cardboard bucket while he stares at the television set. This is
what he had been doing on that quiet evening before the
fateful day.

While jamming fried chicken into his face and
watching a shitty reality show, Peter heard a noise. As far as
he could tell, the noise was coming from outside –
somewhere high above his house, it seemed. It was a loud
whistling, rapidly rising in pitch. Peter briefly paused his
vigorous feeding and cocked his head to the side to listen to
the sound. It was getting louder, as though it were
approaching. Peter shrugged, sending crumbs and grease
flying in all directions. He went back to shoveling chicken
into his gaping mouth.

On the television, a commercial began. Peter grunted,
wiped a beefy hand on his stained T-shirt, and reached for the
remote. Just as he wrapped his thick fingers around the
device, the whistling sound above him reached a crescendo.
Before Peter could muster the energy to get his ass out of the
large recliner, an object crashed through the ceiling right over
his head and sailed across his living room like a cannon ball.

The course of the object sent it smashing directly into the television set with a shattering of glass and an explosion of sparks and smoke.

"Damn," Peter muttered as he sat dumbfounded. He stared at the smoking remnants of his beloved TV, unable to fully comprehend what had just occurred. "Damn," he said again as he reached into the bucket of chicken sitting in his lap. He tore the skin off a drumstick with his teeth and slurped it down his endless gullet. "That was a good show, too," he said, though he could not at all remember what he had just been watching. He gobbled up his chicken leg and prepared to stand up.

Peter is not morbidly obese. He is large – fat, some would say – but not big enough to be considered an invalid. He does, however, have a hard time getting around. He is not very mobile at all, but I suspect that is mostly because he is lazy – incredibly, shockingly, maddeningly lazy.

The unusual nature of the event that had just transpired forced him to reconsider his plans for the evening. Gorging in front of the TV was no longer an option, so with great effort – and an unpleasant series of sounds and smells, Peter hoisted himself out of his chair and shambled over to the ruins of his favorite appliance.

Peter's television, which had died an ignominious and violent death, was very old. It was practically ancient – a floor model that he had inherited from a family member decades before. Peter knelt before the TV's charred corpse. Whatever had crashed through his ceiling was still lodged inside the cabinet. Peter could see it resting on a nest of broken electronic components.

"What is *that* thing?" Peter asked as he bent to get a closer look.

The object was covered in dust. Smoke or vapor rose from it. Peter reached for the object, but pulled back quickly when his fingers got near. The thing was radiating extreme heat. Peter blew a strong breath toward it, clearing off most of the dust to get a better look. When Peter realized what he was looking at, a goofy yelp escaped his lips.

"That's a friggin' satellite!" he cried.

And sure enough, it was. What Peter did not know, though, is that it was a super *secret* satellite that had been placed into orbit by a clandestine organization with a dark, hidden agenda. It had been brought down by another, equally covert group with its own surreptitious machinations using advanced technology unknown and unavailable to the general public. The technology was not perfect. Somehow, the satellite did not vaporize as expected. Instead, it ended up lodged in the television set of a lazy slob named Peter.

Peter studied the satellite visually as it cooled off. He was surprised by how small it was. The satellite was roughly the size and shape of a basketball, metallic silver in color, and adorned with a variety of complex and mysterious scientific instruments.

"I bet that thing is worth a buttload of money," Peter mused aloud. He had a habit of talking to himself, as I'm sure you've noticed. "I wonder if Slick Rick at Mighty Pawn would be interested in it. Maybe I could trade it in for a new TV... one of them fancy flat screen thingies, maybe!"

Well, at the time, it seemed like a great idea to Peter. Don't judge him yet. I'm sure many of you would have thought the same thing, given the circumstances of the peculiar situation. Peter decided to sleep on it. He went to bed with a full belly and a head full of excitement.

That night, Peter had a weird dream. It was most likely caused by his excessive intake of fried chicken that evening, and it is not at all relevant to this story. Curious readers might be interested to know that that the dream featured sea turtles, a magnifying glass, two opera singers dueling over a sandwich, and an appearance from Peter's sixth grade teacher.

In the morning, Peter awoke. He did not yet know it, but he was in for one hell of a day. He got out of bed thinking about pancakes. He had totally forgotten about the satellite still resting inside his television set. He waddled into the kitchen and prepared pancake batter. He took a large, uncooked bowl of the batter into the living room with him. He saw the broken TV.

"Crap," he muttered.

Then he remembered the satellite!

"Oh, yeah," he said.

Peter sat in his chair and ate the entire bowl of pancake batter. He used a chicken bone from the bucket on the floor to scoop it into his mouth. He had actual spoons, but they were in the kitchen and he had no desire to get up again. His expression was vacant, but there was an unusual amount of activity happening within his large, round head. He was contemplating the value of his strange new possession. He was wondering about the satellite's origin. He was even making plans for the day, considering his options, and strategizing. Peter was actually thinking!

By the time he had finished the pancake batter, Peter had formulated a plan. Stepping into action, the first thing he did was retrieve the satellite from the gutted husk of the television. He picked it up carefully, cradling it gently in his hands. He was surprised by the satellite's weight – it was dense and deceptively heavy. Peter carried the object into his bedroom and laid it on his bed. He picked up a sweatshirt from the floor and wrapped the satellite in the soiled, stinky garment. The sweatshirt was green and red and had a picture of a kitten in a Santa Claus hat on the front. Peter wore it often throughout the year. One thing you should know about Peter is that he did not care what people thought of him. This was both a good and a bad thing.

With the satellite wrapped and ready to be transported, Peter got himself dressed. It was about time, too. He had been wearing nothing but greasy underwear for the last two days. He arbitrarily chose an outfit from the heaps of clothing strewn about his bedroom floor. While rooting through the items, he discovered a half-eaten cookie hidden among a pile of socks. He emitted a happy squeal and promptly ate it.

Peter was now ready to embark on the day's adventure! The first stop, he decided, would be the convenience store on the corner. He was in for a workout and he knew he would need calories, so a super-sized fountain drink full of sugary magic would be the perfect companion for a walk downtown to see Slick Rick at Mighty Pawn.

It was a great morning for a walk. Autumn was fast approaching. The heat of the summer was subsiding. Large, billowy clouds drifted overhead and a gentle, aromatic breeze caressed Peter's face. Peter inhaled deeply and smiled as he walked to the convenience store just up the street from his home. He was not aware that the satellite he carried in his hands was, at that very moment, being tracked by two opposing and extremely dangerous factions who would stop at nothing to retrieve the valuable object.

Peter arrived at the neighborhood Suck N' Slurp. He entered and went directly to the soda dispensers at the back of the store. That is where he experienced the first of the day's many misfortunes. To his dismay, there was a handwritten note affixed to the nozzle that dispensed his favorite flavor, Raspberry Spew. The note said: *Out of order – sorry!*

"Oh, come on!" shouted Peter. "Really?"

The cashier at the counter heard him and said, "No Spew today, buddy. Time to try something new, I guess."

It was apparent that the cashier was familiar with Peter and his beverage habits and tastes.

Peter sighed. He pondered his selection before setting the satellite down and grabbing a super-sized cup from the sleeve beside the fountain. He filled the cup with ice and Lemon-Lime Eruption. He slapped a lid on it, inserted a straw, and sipped deeply. It was fizzy, sweet, and good. *Crisis averted*, thought Peter.

Peter went to the counter to pay for his delicious beverage. The cashier, a young man with a purple mohawk and a tattoo of a dragon on his face, yawned as he rang up Peter's purchase.

"That's ninety-seven cents," the cashier said.

Peter awkwardly retrieved his wallet from the front pocket of his pants. The satellite he held to his chest was cumbersome and in the way. The cashier took notice of the object and said, "Whatcha got there?"

"It's nothing," replied Peter as he paid for his drink. "Just some junk I found."

"What kind of junk?"

"Junk junk. It's nothing."

"I bet it's a human head!" The cashier laughed. He had amused himself with that comment.

"It's not a human head. Trust me."

"Can I see it?"

"I... uh... no. I can't. I'm sorry."

Peter quickly shuffled out of the store. As the door was swinging shut behind him, he heard the cashier call out, "If I hear on the news that some dude is missing his head, I'm going to report you!" A hearty laugh followed.

Peter walked on. He had the satellite – still wrapped and concealed in his dirty sweater – under one arm and his Lemon-Lime Eruption in the other hand. Despite the Raspberry Spew disappointment and the obnoxious cashier, he was still in good spirits. He couldn't wait to get to Mighty Pawn. He sipped and walked and walked and sipped. He was feeling just fine.

While Peter enjoyed his stroll, intriguing things were happening somewhere far away. In an underground bunker so secret that even the men who currently occupied it had no idea where they were, a light blinked on a sophisticated, holographic map of the world. The two men monitoring the map sat behind a large console arrayed with advanced computer equipment. The light flashing on the map was a very big deal, but the men showed no emotion.

One of the men activated his headset and spoke: "We have located the birdie. It appears to be intact and at least partially functional. We will continue to track it. Initiate SAT-X 11-17 B protocol, activate re-acquisition sequence, mobilize agents. We need to get to it before *they* do."

Mercifully oblivious to the sinister connotations of the words spoken by the spooky men in the bunker, Peter continued on his way. He was nearing downtown, mere blocks away from Mighty Pawn, when he heard a shout from an approaching car to his left. He turned in the direction of the shout and saw a big, white pickup truck roaring up the street. There was a young man in the passenger seat. He was looking at Peter with a malicious smile on his face. When he noticed that he had gained Peter's attention, he shouted again:

"Weirdo! Loser!"

Before Peter could react, the man in the truck hurled something fast and hard. The driver of the truck accelerated and the vehicle sped away with a thunderous din. The object tumbled through the air and came crashing down right in front of Peter, narrowly missing him. The object exploded when it hit the ground, dowsing Peter in warm liquid. Peter then realized that the man in the truck had thrown a full, plastic bottle at him. The awful reality of what had been in the bottle dawned on him when he could smell and taste the fluid as it trickled down his face and into his mouth.

"Oh, God!" Peter exclaimed. "It's piss!"

It was indeed urine – likely human and likely originating from the bladder of one of the young men in the truck. Who would throw a bottle of piss at an innocent stranger, an unsuspecting pedestrian just out for a stroll and enjoying a fine day? People like the yahoos in that truck, that's who. Every town has them and, unfortunately for Peter, his town has an unusually high concentration of truck-drivin', piss-bottle-throwin', random-insultin' hickified yokels. It's one of the reasons he spends most of his time at home, alone. Don't feel bad, though – Peter has thick skin.

"Ugh," Peter groaned as he used his shirt to wipe the urine from his face. He groaned louder when he realized that he had dropped his massive cup of Lemon-Lime Eruption during the assault. The soda lay in a puddle at his feet, mixing with the nasty yellow fluid that had been in the bottle.

Not to be deterred, Peter regained his composure and continued on his way. He had faced greater challenges than the humiliating episode he had just endured and nothing was going to stop him from getting that satellite into Slick Rick's sleazy, but knowledgeable, hands – at least, that's what he thought then.

Unbeknownst to Peter, an unmarked, black helicopter was, at that very moment, in the air racing to his location. The helicopter carried two very interesting individuals with highly intriguing backgrounds. More about these two individuals will be revealed later, but one thing is abundantly clear: they are serious people on a serious mission, and they are totally intent on retrieving the satellite that Peter is carrying. As you have probably guessed, these individuals are armed with more than bottles of urine.

After walking for more than an hour, Peter finally reached the downtown core of his hometown. The city he lives in is of average size – not a bustling metropolis, but not a village either. In recent years, the city's economy has fallen on hard times and the commercial districts have been in steady decline. Where there were once numerous – and prosperous – family-owned shops and even some big-name retail outlets, now stood mostly pawn shops, liquor stores, and payday loan agencies. It was a travesty, really, but Peter barely took notice. He was not interested in such things.

Peter turned left on May Street. Mighty Pawn was only a few blocks away. Peter allowed himself to visualize all the cool things he could buy if the satellite turned out to be valuable. His limited imagination never strayed far from TV sets, video games, and food. The satellite was, of course, valuable – *very* valuable, in fact – but not in the way that Peter was hoping.

An odd figure shambled up the sidewalk toward him. It was a thin man with one hand pushing a walker and the other holding up his extremely over-sized jeans. The shambling man was shirtless and tanned a deep brown. Wild, bushy hair and a thick, matted beard obscured most of the man's face, except for a pair of wide eyes that peered out like those of a terrified animal fleeing a forest fire. The man appeared to be talking to himself in a low mumble.

As Peter and the man with the walker passed each other, the man's pungent smell caused Peter to quietly gasp and wrinkle his nose. The man noticed this small gesture and promptly screeched loudly in surprise, terror, or just pure and simple madness – probably a little bit of each, I'm sure. The shriek caused Peter to jump and let out a startled cry of his own. The two men screamed in unison for a few weird moments. As the two men went their separate ways, Peter could hear the shambler mutter while he was still in earshot,

"No one likes you. Even God hates you. You're going to die."

That was a disturbing thing to hear! Peter wondered if the comments were directed at him. He then wondered how big of a TV he was going to be able to afford. He also wondered how many chicken nuggets and milkshakes he could buy with the remainder of his imminent windfall. He smiled.

Peter was still smiling when he came to a bus stop with an enclosed shelter. He did not see the woman standing inside until she spoke:

"Hi, honey. Looking for a date?"

Leaning against the inside wall of the shelter was a very large woman in a fur coat... at least, that is what Peter saw at first glance. Upon closer inspection, Peter realized that the thick, gaudy makeup and obvious wig masked distinctly masculine features. Stubble was clearly visible on the person's face, and Peter could even see an Adam's apple peeking through the lapels of the fur coat. Peter was not offended nor disgusted, but he replied to the solicitation honestly.

"Oh, no, thank you," he said. "I'm not gay."

A look of mortified shock appeared on the bulky transvestite's face. "Well, neither am *I*, honey!" she cried. "Are you insinuating that I am a *man*? Do I *look* like a man to you?"

Peter was in a predicament. He stammered and stumbled over his words as he tried to find the correct response. Unfortunately, for him, there *was* no correct response. Whatever he said was only going to make it worse. He did not know this, however, and made a valiant attempt to extricate himself from the awkward situation.

"I'm sorry," Peter said. "No offense intended... I just assumed..."

"You just assumed *what*, exactly?"

"That, you know, you were a, um... you know, male hooker. I'm not judging you!"

"So, just because of a little harmless flirting you assume I'm a *prostitute*? How dare you. You haven't been with many women, have you?"

"I really haven't. I'm sorry."

The situation quickly escalated when, from behind the bus shelter, a short man dressed entirely in brown leather popped out. Even the man's fedora hat was apparently made of brown leather. The man swaggered over to stand beside the transvestite. A thin mustache graced the man's upper lip, from below which jutted a huge cigar that reeked of cheap hotels and sleazy bars.

"Is this bandejo giving you a hard time, Cupcake?" the little man asked.

"This prick called me a tranny whore, Felipe," replied Cupcake.

"I didn't say that," Peter said. "I think there's been a misunderstanding."

"Are you calling Cupcake a *liar?*" asked Felipe with a malignant scowl. "I think you owe her an apology, cabron."

"I'm sorry, Cupcake. Really, I am."

"Sure," scoffed Cupcake, looking away.

"Whatcha got there?" Felipe asked, referring to the satellite Peter cradled in his arms, still wrapped in his Christmas kitty sweater.

"This? Oh, it's nothing."

"Looks like something to me, sweetheart," Cupcake said. "Why don't you let us have a look?"

Peter hesitated. Cupcake reached for the satellite. Felipe pulled a switchblade out of his pocket. He released the blade with the push of a button and held the weapon menacingly.

"I think you better let my lady have a look,

homeboy," Felipe sneered.

The moment was tense, the danger palpable. Peter understood that his options were limited. He considered running. He considered yelling for help. Instead, he chose to do what seemed to be the only sensible thing – he started unwrapping the satellite. Cupcake and Felipe leaned in expectantly. Peter slowly peeled away the sweater. Cupcake and Felipe were on the figurative edge of their seats. Their eyes grew wide. Their anticipation increased.

Just as Peter was about to fully reveal the mysterious object, the satellite suddenly came to life. It emitted a series of shrill beeps. Small LED lights on its metallic silver exterior began flashing in an enigmatic sequence. Cupcake and Felipe jumped back in terror.

"It's a bomb!" Cupcake shrieked.

"This dude is *loco!*" cried Felipe. "Run, Kenny! Get the fuck out of here!" In his panic, Felipe had inadvertently referred to Cupcake by the name she had been given at birth. It was a natural mistake.

Cupcake and Felipe got the fuck out of there in a hurry. Peter watched in disbelief as the pair ran up the sidewalk into a large bush like two children who had just seen a rabid, mutant hellhound. The satellite in his hands continued beeping loudly. The lights around its circumference flashed and flickered. Peter stared at the device, fascinated.

Many miles away, the men in the black helicopter monitored a screen mounted to the dashboard of the highly advanced aircraft. The signal they had been watching had suddenly changed. The small, dim blip had become a large, rapidly pulsing orb.

"We have increased activity," the co-pilot said to the pilot. "Looks like the birdie has awakened."

Ominous!

Just as suddenly as it had burst to life, the satellite in Peter's hands went silent and the lights ceased flashing. The loud and dazzling display was now over. Peter did not speculate on the meaning of what had just occurred. He simply wrapped the satellite up again in the old sweater.

Just ahead, at the end of the block, Peter could see the brown brick facade of Mighty Pawn, the largest pawn shop in the city and the primary destination of our intrepid adventurer on this atypical and lively day. Peter, as is his way, was able to almost instantly brush off the unsettling encounter with Cupcake and Felipe and go about his business. His resilience is admirable, but his testing is not yet over.

What more could possible happen before Peter finally reaches the pawn shop, you might ask? Much, *much* more, actually. He could step into an open manhole, for instance. A bird could poop on him, or a dog could appear out of nowhere and bite him on the rear. Have you ever tripped on a crack in the sidewalk? It's very embarrassing when people are watching. Any of these things could happen to him, couldn't they? Something outlandish could occur – something so bizarre that even in the context of this story, it would be difficult to swallow. He could simply run into someone he really doesn't want to see. Well, none of these things happened.

After a few uneventful yards, Peter finally arrived at Mighty Pawn. He pushed open the heavy, reinforced door and stepped in. Even for one who has visited before, entering Mighty Pawn can be quite an experience. The sheer amount of *stuff* inside boggles the mind. The building itself covers nearly half of a city block, and practically every square inch of its voluminous interior is occupied by used merchandise. It is a junk lover's Mecca, a knick-knack fanatic's dream, a second-hand paradise.

One must squeeze through overflowing racks of power tools upon entering. This was a challenge for our rotund friend Peter, but he did so as carefully as he could. He passed through the first gauntlet and arrived at the electronics section, a chaotic jumble of devices and appliances arranged in vague categories – a stack of DVD players in one area, stacked TVs in another, and microwaves, blenders, toasters, and other contraptions piled in disorderly fashion in all available spaces. Claustrophobia clawed at Peter's brain, which was on the verge of total sensory overload, but he fought it off and bravely soldiered on.

Peter successfully traversed the electronics department and found himself among racks of DVDs and CDs – thousands of them, it seemed. Row upon row, it was as if Might Pawn had a copy, or multiple copies, of every single movie and album that had ever been released. This was Peter's favorite section. He practically salivated at the thought of all the hours of entertainment contained within these walls. We know Peter really enjoys food, but he gets nearly as much pleasure from some good ol' watchin', and there sure was some quality watchin' material gathered on the shelves of Mighty Pawn! Browsing would have to wait until another visit, though. Peter was still on a mission.

"Can I help you?"

The question snapped Peter's reverie. He wiped his drooling mouth and said, "Huh?"

"Can I help you? Are you looking for something?"

The man who addressed Peter was standing behind a large counter at the back of the pawn shop. It was Slick Rick, Peter realized. This was the man he had walked all the way downtown to see. The walls on either side of the counter were covered in gun racks. Semi-automatic rifles of a multitude of varieties hung on the racks, giving this section of the shop the appearance of an armory. The counter behind which Slick Rick stood also served as a glass display case. The display case was full of handguns.

Peter approached the counter as Slick Rick polished a lethal-looking, military-style rifle. You might not be surprised to find out that Slick Rick is quite a character himself. At 300 pounds, he is shockingly even larger than Peter. An NRA T-shirt barely contained his bulging gut, and his substantial arms jiggled like a seal's belly as he stroked the weapon. He kept his hair short and his face clean-shaven, so his oval head looked somewhat like a giant egg perched on a skin pillow – the skin pillow being his abnormally massive neck, of course.

"I have something I thought you might be interested in," said Peter. "I think it could be worth a lot of money."

"Is that so?" replied Slick Rick. "Well, I'll be the judge of that."

Peter laid his bundle on the counter and peeled away the sweater. Slick Rick kept his eyes on the rifle he was cleaning and showed no interest in what Peter was presenting to him.

"I think it's a satellite," Peter said. "You know, from space or some shit. It crashed into my TV. Look at all these fancy thingies on it. It's gotta be worth something, right?"

Despite Slick Rick's feigned ambivalence, Peter's words managed to intrigue him enough that he momentarily stopped what he was doing and glanced over at the object sitting on the counter. After getting a glimpse, he quickly resumed the ritualistic and highly suggestive act of cleaning the large rifle.

"Hmm," muttered Slick Rick. "Interesting. So what do you want for it? Keep in mind that the thing is probably broken, and there's really not much of a market for satellites, you know."

"I need a new TV. I was hoping to get one of those nice flat screen models."

"Ha," scoffed Slick Rick. "I doubt this thing is worth *that* much."

The truth is, Slick Rick was highly interested in the rare and unusual piece of technology. If it was indeed what he suspected it might be, he knew of people in underground, deep black markets who would pay generously for such a device. It was not the first time an object of enigmatic origin had appeared in his shop. Petrified dinosaur eggs, prosthetic limbs, shrunken heads, and religious artifacts had all, at one time or another, passed through the Mighty Pawn doors. Someone once tried to pawn a toilet seat that Richard Nixon had supposedly sat on while in office... but that's another story.

In *this* story, things are about to take a turn for the surreal. You've stuck with me this far, and I appreciate that, so bear with me while this tale resolves itself in the only appropriate way. Hang on – it could get a little zany.

As Slick Rick was being his usual slick self, a startling transformation occurred. Right in front of Peter's eyes, in the middle of their conversation, Slick Rick's demeanor suddenly changed. His face went slack and his mouth fell open. His body sagged and he dropped the rag that he had been using to polish the gun. His eyes assumed a spooky, distant quality, as if someone had simply turned out the lights. It was like instant catatonia.

"Hey," Peter said, "are you alright?"

Like an abandoned shell, Rick remained motionless and unresponsive. Peter began to get nervous. He reached over, gently poked Slick Rick in the shoulder and said, "Um, hello? Are you in there?"

Slick Rick jolted at the touch. He suddenly sat up on the stool on which he had been seated, his back rigid, his posture stiff. His huge, round head wobbled as his now bulging, protuberant eyes struggled to focus on what was in front of him. His fat lips flapped grotesquely as his mouth attempted to form words. Peter observed this freaky development with slight concern. He thought perhaps Slick Rick was suffering from a bad case of heartburn, or at the worst, a minor stroke. He was wrong on both counts – oh, so very, very wrong.

"Rick, buddy... you don't look so good. Should I call an ambulance?"

Slick Rick's lips ceased flapping and his eyes locked on Peter's with furious intensity. He spoke, but the voice that boomed out of his throat was no longer his own:

"Fool! It is *you* who will require the ambulance – and a body bag!"

"What? Why? I just thought we were negotiating."

"Idiot! Imbecile! You have no idea what you have gotten yourself into, do you? You shall soon pay for your folly."

"I thought we were cool, Rick. I know I'm not a *regular* customer, but I've given you my fair share of business."

"Rick is dead, you ignorant heap of feces."

The entity that had assumed control of Slick Rick's body reached for the satellite and said, "For the glory of the hive, the device is ours once again!"

Peter reacted with surprising swiftness. He snatched the satellite just before the entity's hands closed around it. It was quick thinking and a smooth move. His mother would have been proud of him.

"I don't know what the hell is going on around here," Peter said," but I think I should hold on to this for now."

"Foolish mortal!" the entity bellowed. "We're going to suck the soul out of your meat and throw your carcass to the drones!"

Peter didn't like the sound of that. He started toward

the exit, clutching the satellite close to his chest. Behind him now, the entity rose from the stool. It had every intention of pursuing and incapacitating Peter, but, unfortunately for the entity, it had chosen to inhabit the body of a very unhealthy man.

Grunting and wheezing, the entity attempted to maneuver the cumbersome flesh vessel out from behind the counter. It was an ordeal! The entity managed to squeeze past the counter, but it underestimated the true girth of the man it wore. Slick Rick's gigantic ass slammed into a rack of ammunition, which toppled over onto a life-size mannequin in full tactical gear. The mannequin bounced against a wall before falling into the glass display counter. The display counter shattered, sending glass fragments flying in all directions. As the entity tried to maintain its balance, it slipped on the glass and fell to the floor with an audible splat.

The sound of the commotion caused Peter to stop. He turned to see the entity rolling around helplessly on the floor. It was trying to get back to its feet, but the excess flesh made it extremely difficult. It flopped and flailed like a beached sea beast. It was a pathetic sight.

"Are you hurt?" Peter asked.

"We're going to eat your eyeballs and devour your guts!" the entity screeched. "We're going to guzzle your blood and gobble your brains!"

"Do you need some help getting up?"

"Fool! Even as I speak, more of us are coming. You'll never leave this place alive!"

There was truth to that statement. What Peter did not know is that just outside, two people were waiting for him – two familiar people, in fact. Here's a hint: One of them is a large and very masculine-looking woman, the other is a small, Hispanic man dressed entirely in brown leather. They are not who they once were, however.

A mile away and closing in fast, the men in the black helicopter continued to track the mysterious device that had instigated this weird saga. The blip on their monitor, which indicated the satellite's position, had been joined by three other blinking lights.

"We have hive activity in the area," the co-pilot said.

"We will be at the target in less than a minute," said the pilot. "Prepare to touch down. Get ready to fight."

Inside Mighty Pawn, Peter decided that he had had enough of Slick Rick's colorful and gruesome threats. He would take his business elsewhere, thank you very much.

Peter stepped through the door with the precious bundle tucked under his arm. The entities who inhabited Felipe and Kenny... er, *Cupcake*, were waiting in ambush. As soon as Peter appeared on the sidewalk, Cupcake seized him from behind. She held him tightly in her formidable grip as Felipe rushed at him with his blade raised.

"Disgusting mortal!" cried the thing that inhabited Felipe. "That object you hold in your stinking hands is more valuable than your feeble brain could possibly comprehend. Give it to me now and I will kill you quickly."

"Geez," said Peter. "If you want it that bad, you can have it. I just wanted a new TV."

"Poke his eyes out," snarled Cupcake's entity-possessor. "Fillet his face. I hate being in this rotten bag of meat. He needs to pay for this."

Felipe's entity nodded thoughtfully and said, "That's not a bad idea. It's been a while since I've tortured a human being. I should do it just for old times' sake. Remember all the fun we used to have in the early days of the war, before it got stale? Those were good times."

"Whoa, buddy," Peter protested, "you don't need to do that. Just take the damn thing. I don't want it anymore. It's been nothing but trouble since I found it. Please, just take it."

"Start with his scalp," suggested Cupcake.

Felipe leaned in with his switchblade poised. Just as he was about to begin peeling away Peter's scalp and rather greasy hair, the loud whirring of an approaching helicopter caused him, as well as Cupcake and Peter, to look up in unison. The unmarked, black aircraft was coming in from the north fast. It began its descent – headed directly toward the trio gathered outside Mighty Pawn. Cupcake briefly relaxed her grip, allowing Peter to pull away.

"It's *them*," Felipe muttered.

"How did they get here so fast?" Cupcake said. "They must have upgraded their tracking capabilities."

Peter, meanwhile, began to walk calmly away. He did not care about the helicopter or the apparent battle for the mysterious machine. He just wanted to go home. After a day like he'd had, who could blame him?

"The mortal! Stop him!" shouted Cupcake.

Peter slowly turned and placed the satellite on the pavement. He let out a long, deep sigh. "It's yours," he said. "Just let me go. I'm hungry and tired."

"Forget about him," Felipe said. "We don't have time to waste torturing some random *Unaware*. Get the device."

Cupcake rushed over and scooped up the satellite. The helicopter was nearly on top of them now. Felipe had dropped his switchblade and had raised his arms high above his head in a show of defiance. He shook his balled fists at the helicopter and shouted unintelligibly. Peter turned and continued walking up the sidewalk toward home. Cupcake watched him for a moment before turning her attention to the rapidly descending helicopter, the rotors of which were stirring up dirt and debris as it closed in. It stopped and hovered right in front of Felipe.

A loudspeaker mounted on the helicopter crackled to life and a booming voice proclaimed, "There is nowhere to run. Set the device down and move away from it. Failure to comply will result in your destruction."

"Human filth!" shouted Felipe. "You will never destroy us. We are eternal! We are Legion!"

Peter ignored the exciting scene behind him and casually strolled away. He was already planning his afternoon snack, which he would thoroughly enjoy just as soon as he got home.

What Peter did not see was fairly remarkable. The entity inhabiting Felipe had begun summoning balls of brilliant, purple plasma energy with his raised hands. He was flinging them at the hovering helicopter. Cupcake had somehow manifested a force field, which she used to shield herself and the device. The helicopter, rocking each time it was hit with a plasma ball, fired blue laser beams at the entities on the ground from a weapon mounted beneath the cockpit. It was a brutal firefight to the death, in broad daylight, right in front of Mighty Pawn.

While the battle raged behind him, Peter rubbed his eyes and yawned. It had been a rough day and he still had a fairly long walk ahead of him. He no longer had a television set, but he wasn't too upset about that any more. He decided that when he got home, he was going to eat an entire pizza while reading comic books. He had earned it.

Ballena

In San Francisco's bustling financial district, the light of the sun rarely reaches the street. Skyscrapers dominate, towering over the pedestrians and motorists like monolithic guardians of steel and concrete. Around noon, when the swarming crowds winding through the labyrinthine streets are thickest, the sun casts its rays ambivalently upon the throngs of people below.

The masses move like rats in a maze, each individual in pursuit of his or her own little piece of the cheese. Among them now, on a typical weekday in mid-summer, is a man named Jonas. Jonas is a 35-year-old bank clerk. He is on his lunch break and he is very hungry. He is on his way to his favorite Chinese restaurant to get something spicy, filling, and affordable. As he works his way up the congested sidewalk, Jonas observes the other pedestrians around him with a cold, cynical eye. He is completely surrounded by people, yet he feels totally alone.

As he approaches an intersection, Jonas passes a man wearing headphones, apparently listening to hip hop. The man is yelling along to the music with no care or concern for those around him. The man charges past Jonas, spouting crude and violent lyrics, his face distorted in a hostile scowl. Jonas sighs. The street rappers and their intrusive public performances are common. Jonas has had a hard week and is feeling irritable. "Just shut up," he mutters. "No one wants to hear that shit."

Jonas comes to a stop and stands with the others waiting at the corner for the light to cross. With few exceptions, everyone around him is staring at their cell phones and, like the rapper, listening to music through headphones nestled in their ears. They are plugged into their own worlds, essentially oblivious to their surroundings. They only act and react as programmed. When the light changes, the little walking man on the sign begins to flash and they cross the street like a herd of cattle.

On the other side of the street, a homeless man is sitting cross-legged on the corner. His clothes are tattered and his face is blackened with filth. A hand-scrawled sign is propped up against the man's knees and he is holding out a large Styrofoam cup.

"Can you spare something for a vet, brother?" the homeless man asks.

"I don't have any money on me," Jonas replies honestly. "I'm sorry."

"Yeah right, asshole," the homeless man sneers.

Jonas is only a few minutes walk away from Chinatown, where his favorite restaurant is located. He is eager to get out of the financial district. He picks up his pace and practically jogs up the hill that will take him to the Dragon's Gate – the entrance to Chinatown and a passageway into another culture, another world, another time – a unique and mysterious district that exists like another dimension directly in the heart of the city.

Jonas reaches the archway over the sidewalk. As he passes through, he places his hand on the large dragon statue standing to his right like a silent, vigilant sentinel. It is his custom to do so – he believes it is good luck.

"Hey there, big guy," Jonas says. "Here I am again. Another day, another dollar."

Moving on, Jonas continues up the sidewalk which, like many in San Francisco, rises before him at a steep angle. He allows himself to soak up the oriental ambiance as he walks. For the moment, at least, the stress of his job and the

crushing pressure of the populous city are far behind him.
Although he visits Chinatown at least once a week, Jonas still
feels like he has been transported to the other side of the
planet when he passes through the gate.

A multitude of shops and markets line the street,
selling toys, fireworks, souvenirs, vegetables, tobacco, liquor,
and nearly every conceivable variety of sea creature. The fish
vendors never fail to surprise Jonas with what some people
find delectable, let alone edible. The street is alive with
activity, though it is of a much different type than that in the
financial district. Aside from the tourists, who often bring
with them a loud and boisterous energy, the locals live and
work in a quiet, efficient, productive ebb and flow. The
merchants are busy stocking their displays and sweeping up
around their shops and stands. The local shoppers and
pedestrians move through the neighborhood along routine
paths, focused and content.

As Jonas walks past one of the many gift shops, an
object on a shelf loaded with trinkets catches his eye through
a propped-open door. Jonas stops walking and
uncharacteristically decides to step into the shop to get a
better look. The machinery of destiny whirs into action.

Jonas picks up the object, a small, ceramic dragon
with Chinese characters painted on its side. It had been
sitting on a shelf with other animal trinkets, each signifying
one of the 12 Chinese zodiacal years. Jonas feels an instant
and usual attachment to the object in his hands. A strange
emotion stirs within him, a potent mixture of longing,
nostalgia, and deep affection. He thinks of his wife Nadine,
who had been born in the Year of the Dragon. Life had
recently been hectic and difficult for the two of them. Too
much work and too little time maintaining their relationship
had taken its toll. They had been drifting apart.

"How much for this little dragon?" Jonas asks the old

man sitting on a stool behind the counter and reading a newspaper. "My wife would love it."

"Ten dollars," the man responds. "Cash."

Jonas studies the tiny statue and ponders its value. On impulse, he pulls a bill out of his wallet and pays for it. The shopkeeper wraps it up and puts it in a gift box. Jonas takes the box, leaves the shop, and continues up the street toward his favorite restaurant. He now has an excited bounce in his step. He can't wait to get home after work and surprise his wife with the gift.

Jonas enjoys a bowl of noodles and returns to work, distracted and distant, ready to finish his shift. After work, he gets on the freeway and begins the long commute to his home in the suburbs. It is Friday and the traffic is even more congested than usual. The endless stream of cars creeps slowly, excruciatingly slowly, north. Jonas studies the faces of the commuters around him. Nearly everyone has the same exasperated, tense expression. Stop, start, creep, and crawl – the drive home is an agonizing ordeal.

Finally at home, Jonas stumbles through the front door. He has the small box with the ceramic dragon in his hand. Nadine is waiting for him in the kitchen. "Hi, honey," she says when she sees him. "You look like the walking dead. The good news is we're having brains for dinner tonight."

Jonas manages a weak chuckle. He gives Nadine a kiss on the top of her head and then collapses into a seat at the kitchen table. "I have a little something for you," he says as he hands her the box. "I couldn't resist."

"Aw! That's sweet. I remember when we used to get little gifts for each other all the time. Thank you."

Nadine opens the box. She pulls out the tiny statue and smiles. Her eyes water up. "It's perfect. I love it," she says.

"I saw it on my lunch break and immediately thought

of you. Actually, I've been thinking a lot about us today. I'm sure you know that I've been stressed out a lot lately. I know you have been, too. It's like all we do is drive, work, drive, eat, sleep, repeat. It seems like there's never any time for *us*."

"I know what you mean," Nadine nods. "I miss you. I miss our conversations. I miss laughing and having fun."

"Why don't we take off this weekend? Tomorrow. Let's just get in the car and drive somewhere, *anywhere* – get out of the house, get out of the city. We'll find a quiet spot on the beach, put our feet in the ocean, and drink wine while we watch the sunset. How does that sound?"

"That sounds like a dream."

The next morning, Jonas and Nadine do exactly that. They load up the car with supplies and hit the highway, elated by the spirit of adventure and the thrill of the unknown that awaits them on the road. They are unaware that the machinery of destiny continues to whir behind the scenes, that they are about to be thrust into the jaws of danger.

Two hours into their journey, Jonas and Nadine are driving up the coast with the sounds and smells of the ocean drifting through the open car windows. To their left, beyond the guard rail, the terrain drops off steeply – a sharp slope merges with the roiling, white-tipped waves of the sea as it crashes against the shore. The Pacific reaches the horizon, beyond which is land they have only visited in their imaginations – the islands of Japan and the vast continent of Asia. The young couple lives in the Now, thoroughly engrossed in the present they are creating, delighting in each other's company and the beauty of their surroundings.

"This was a great idea," Nadine says as she leans back in the passenger seat and puts her feet on the dashboard. "I haven't seen another car or person for miles. It's like we're the only ones left on the planet."

"Maybe we are," replies Jonas. "Maybe we got out of

town just in time to miss the Apocalypse. Or maybe we slipped through a portal and ended up in an alternate reality. Either way, it's nice. I like it."

"If something like that were true, there are very few people I'd miss," Nadine says with a shake of her head and a hearty laugh. She pauses while gathering her thoughts. The open road always makes her contemplative, philosophical. When she speaks again, her tone is serious and reflective:

"Do you ever get the feeling that you are totally out of sync with the world? Lately I've been finding it hard to relate to the people around me – co-workers, friends, even some of my family – everyone seems so self-absorbed, so egotistical, so petty and competitive."

"The funny thing is," Jonas adds, "everyone is thinking the same way, dressing the same way, watching the same movies and TV shows, playing the same games. Have you noticed how little tolerance most people have for people they don't agree with? It's a hard time to be an individual. I have sympathy for the young people who are still trying to discover who they really are in this bizarre, new world."

"That's why I can't be bothered with social media anymore. The rampant narcissism and obvious polarization turn me off. Technology should *serve* humans, yet it seems like, in many ways, people are slaves to their devices."

Jonas eyes his wife with love and admiration. "You're firing on all cylinders today, baby. I like it. Your mind turns me on."

"Well, all this deep thought is making me hungry. Do you feel like stopping somewhere for a bite to eat?"

"There's a sign just ahead. Let's see what it says. We'll find a place to take a break, get some food, and stretch our legs."

Within moments, a sign conveniently appears. It informs the couple that they are mere miles from a place called Ballena.

"Ballena," says Jonas. "Never heard of it. Must be a really small town."

"Sounds vaguely familiar to me," Nadine says. "I think it's a fishing village on the coast. Could be a cool place to check out."

Jonas and Nadine are deeply nestled in the groove of fate as it leads them up the highway. They pull off at the exit that will take them to Ballena, blissfully ignorant of what awaits them. Their adventure has just begun.

The tiny, coastal town of Ballena sits at the southern edge of a peninsula that juts and curves into the Pacific Ocean, creating a bay that is largely unknown to the general public. Jonas and Nadine are driving on the rough road that they expect will lead them to the town center. They look for signs of civilization or habitation, but see none of that. Instead, it is as if they have arrived on an alien planet. The terrain has abruptly and dramatically changed. Between the road and the beach, the land undulates, the soil shifting in shades of dark gray and black, sparsely punctuated by unusual, twisted bushes. Bizarre, brightly-colored plants jut from the ground in intermittent patches like the tentacles of a buried leviathan.

"Look at those plants!" cries Nadine. "I've never seen anything like them."

"Quite pretty," Jonas says. "It's very scenic around here."

"The vegetation is fascinating, but also kinda grotesque. I'm a little spooked, to be honest. Shouldn't there be a sign somewhere to indicate where the town is?"

"Maybe the townsfolk don't *want* to be found. Ballena could be California's best-kept secret. It could be paradise, Shangri-La, a hidden utopia."

"Yeah, right. It's probably a town full of '60s rejects –

psychedelic hippie casualties. They're probably trying to hide their pot farms."

Just up the road, a crude, wooden sign has been nailed to a post at the side of the road. When the car nears, Nadine reads the text out loud:

"*Welcome to Ballena. Now please turn around and go away. Love and peace be with you.* Well, isn't that charming. The tourism board should really work on that slogan."

"You were right," smiles Jonas. "Just a bunch of happy and harmless hippies with a sense of humor. They're probably trying to scare off the straights."

"*I'm* a little scared."

"Don't be silly. We're on an adventure. Let's find some food and have some fun."

Jonas and Nadine continue up the road. Not far past the sign, they finally see evidence of the town – a few old, decrepit buildings. They appear to be in serious disrepair, but upon closer inspection, Nadine and Jonas realize that they are, in fact, inhabited. A shirtless, bearded man sits on the porch of one of the homes and eyes their car coldly, suspiciously, as they drive past.

"*He* looked friendly," Nadine jokes.

"Probably just stoned," laughs Jonas.

The road leads the couple past the small cluster of decaying homes at the edge of town and into what serves as the city center – essentially a handful of shops and restaurants in only marginally better shape then the houses they just passed. The road leads right through town and directly to the ocean, which Jonas and Nadine can clearly see just ahead of them, blue and white, glistening in the sun.

The car rolls slowly down the street. Jonas spots a building with a large, grinning, cartoon crab painted on its exterior. The paint is peeling and the building itself looks like it should have been condemned sometime in the early '70s.

Jonas is not deterred. He points to it and says, "There's a restaurant. I bet they have great seafood. Let's go try their clam chowder."

"You want to eat *there?*" Nadine asks incredulously.

"Yeah! Come on," Jonas urges. "Where's your spirit of adventure? This is our getaway trip. You only live once, remember?"

"And I want to continue living. When do you think a health inspector last walked through the door of *that* place? I can only imagine what goes on in that kitchen. Makes me shudder to think about it."

"You're kind of bringing me down. This was supposed to be a fun trip."

"You're right. I'm sorry. This place just creeps me out a bit. I'm sure the food will be fine. Should be fresh at the very least, right? Let's check it out. I *am* hungry."

"That's the spirit!"

Jonas parks the car and he and Nadine step out. It is just after noon and the street is virtually empty and eerily silent. An emaciated dog with crusty fur trots up the middle of the street in search of scraps. An elderly man in a black suit and tie sits on a bench across the street staring into space with a blank expression on his gaunt face. A gentle breeze blows through the street, carrying with it the rich, salty scent of the ocean. Jonas approaches the restaurant door, half expecting it to be nailed shut. He turns the knob and the door opens.

A bell above the door rings as Jonas and Nadine enter. In contrast to the dilapidated state of the exterior, the interior of the restaurant is warm, tidy, and inviting. The entire room has been decorated in an aquatic motif. Various nautical implements, including ships' wheels and oars, hang on the brown and red wood-paneled walls along with paintings and photographs depicting all varieties of ocean life. The restaurant is spacious and well-maintained. A door at the far end leads to the kitchen, from which a male voice now calls out: "That you, Ernie? Why don't you come back later. I ain't got time for your shit."

Jonas and Nadine look at each other, amused. "Hi, there," Jonas says loudly. "Are you open for business?"

A moment of silence lapses, followed by faint muttering, possible cursing, and the clatter of pots and pans. Jonas and Nadine wait for a response. They are beginning to feel awkward. Finally the door to the kitchen swings open and a man appears. The man is short, frail, and very old. He is wearing a grease-spattered white T-shirt, dirty blue jeans, and a sailor's cap, which sits at a skewed angle upon a wily mass of silvery hair. Naval tattoos cover the old man's thin arms. His face is deeply lined and incredibly tanned. A cigarette dangles from his pursed lips and remains in position even when he speaks: "Actual customers! Well, I'll be damned. You folks tourists? I ain't served no one but locals in a long time... a *very* long time indeed."

"Is it that obvious?" Nadine smiles. "Yes, we're just passing through. My husband was in the mood for some clam chowder and, well, this seemed like the right place to get some."

"You got that right, lady! Best damn chowder in the country, I reckon. Come on in and have a seat. The name's Elvis, like the singer... but don't remind me of that because I hate that punk greaser and his so-called music."

Jonas laughs and says, "Fair enough! Was never much of a fan myself." He and Nadine take a seat at a table in the middle of the restaurant.

"You folks from the city?" Elvis asks as he arranges napkins, dishes, and silverware in front of the diners.

"We are, yes," replies Nadine. "We're on a much-needed vacation. It feels good to get away. This is a lovely area."

"I don't blame ya!" Elvis cries. "I can't stand the big city. Haven't been there since I served in the war. Is it still full of hippies and queers?"

Jonas chuckles nervously. "It's a diverse and dynamic city. I'm sure a lot has changed since your last visit."

"Change isn't always a good thing," Elvis says. "I've seen a lot of change in my life and most of it was for the worse. The world is going to Hell in a handbasket and I'm too old to care. Anyway, enough of my complaining. I'm just a crotchety, old fart. You two seem like a nice, young couple. What else can I get ya with your soup? You will love it, by the way. It's delicious. I'm not boasting – that's just a *fact.*"

"I'll take a coffee, please," Nadine says.

"Me, too," nods Jonas.

"You got it," Elvis grins. He saunters back to the kitchen and returns promptly with a fresh pot of coffee. He fills two cups and says, "I'll be back in a jiffy with your soup. Please relax and enjoy yourselves."

Elvis returns to the kitchen, whistling. When the door shuts behind him, Nadine shakes her head and says, "Well, *he's* a real character. I don't know *what* to make of him."

"Aw, he's a nice enough old guy. He's just set in his ways. I kinda like him."

Jonas and Nadine spend the short wait for their soup engaged in easy, comfortable conversation, enjoying their time together away from the city. They are immersed in the moment in the cozy, charming, and timeless atmosphere of the restaurant. Elvis soon returns to the table with two full bowls of hearty, steaming soup on a tray. He carefully places a bowl in front of each of the eager diners.

"Enjoy your food," Elvis says, "and I hope you enjoy your stay in Ballena, too. Are you planning on staying the night?"

"Probably not," replies Jonas. "This is just a day trip and there's more we want to see up the coast."

"Good," Elvis says gravely, with a touch of relief. "This is a nice town to visit, but I don't recommend an extended stay. In fact, I would strongly urge you to move on as quickly as you can. Have your meal, enjoy your stay, but be on your way before the sun goes down. This is not somewhere you want to be stuck for the night. Trust me."

Elvis wanders back to the kitchen, leaving Jonas and Nadine to ponder his vague, cryptic warning. Jonas breaks the tension with a shrug and a smile. "He's just trying to spook us," he says, spooning soup into his mouth. "They don't take too kindly to strangers in these parts."

"It worked," Nadine says. "I'm spooked."

Jonas and Nadine finish eating and pay for their food. When the transaction is completed, Elvis thanks them and says, "Remember what I said about leaving town before dark. I like you kids. Stay safe."

The couple leaves the restaurant. The street is still strangely devoid of activity. Even the man in the black suit who had been sitting on the bench has disappeared. Jonas and Nadine stand alone, like the last survivors of a silent, unseen cataclysm, the orphaned leftovers of a vanished race. It has been a weird day, but Jonas is still in good spirits. "Let's go to the beach," he says. "We need to see the ocean."

Nadine agrees and they begin the short walk up the street that will lead them directly to the water's edge. As they get closer, new sounds intermingle with the roaring and crashing of waves, indistinguishable at first, but rising in volume and gaining clarity upon approach. At the crest of a small hill that slopes down to meet the ocean, Jonas and Nadine spot the source of the sounds – a large congregation of people gathered by the shore.

"Wow, look at 'em all," Jonas says. "Now I know why

the town seemed deserted – everyone's partying on the beach."

The scene does indeed resemble a party. There are men and women, mostly young, fit, and scantily clad, swimming, surfing, playing volleyball, and sunbathing. A large group sits around a huge, stone fire pit on the beach, playing guitars, hand drums, and tambourines. The pleasant tones of a folk song rise from the musicians, providing a serene, yet haunting soundtrack to the festivities.

"Feel like crashing a party?" Jonas grins.

"I don't know if we'd be welcome," replies Nadine.

"They look friendly enough to me! It's all part of the adventure, right?"

"Alright, I suppose. Just don't drink the Kool-Aid, okay?"

"Tune in, turn on, and drop out, baby. Can you dig it?"

Where the road ends, Nadine follows Jonas as he descends the concrete steps that lead down to the beach. Although she trusts her husband, she feels a slight reluctance, a subtle dread. Jonas can be impulsive, but he has never in the past gotten them into serious trouble. As she observes the scene on display before her, however, Nadine senses something dark lurking behind the revelry – something ominous concealed in the festivities. She briefly visualizes Hieronymus Bosch's beautiful and unsettling masterpiece *The Garden of Earthly Delights*. She considers asking Jonas to rethink his decision to approach the party, but it is too late. He is already on the beach. Nadine joins him and takes his hand.

Jonas and Nadine stroll through the sand toward the water's edge. The people gathered on the beach accept them into their midst with gentle smiles and sincere greetings. A peaceful, joyful mood pervades the scene. When the couple reaches the spot near the water where the dark, wet sand indicates the furthest reaches of the tide, they sit down on the dry sand just above it. Jonas wraps an arm around Nadine and she folds into his embrace. A seagull lands on a large piece of driftwood sticking out of the sand and studies the couple with a raw and peculiar intelligence glinting in its eyes.

"I could live like this," Jonas says. "Just quit my job and become a beach bum. The bank sure wouldn't miss me. What do you think?"

"You'll have to learn how to surf," replies Nadine. "Maybe Elvis would hire you to wash dishes."

"Nah, I'd just catch my own food and cook it right here. In all seriousness, though, I miss when life was *simpler*. It's hard to accept that soon we'll be back in the grind with all the other sad souls. Traffic, pollution, crime, politics, bills, taxes, drudgery, and death... ugh."

"It's really depressing when you put it that way. We should be thankful for what we have. Don't you appreciate all that we have worked to achieve?"

"I do. I really do. We have a nice home in a nice neighborhood. You like your job and, for the most part, I like mine. I guess part of me envies those – like the people here on the beach – who seem to have few responsibilities and little or no stress in their lives."

"And probably no ambition or goals. Is that really how you want to live? Like that piece of driftwood, just carried along with the tide? I thought you had direction and drive. It's your determination to *make* something of yourself that I admire. The city – and society itself – is complex and crazy. I know that, but the system has also given us the opportunity to *improve* our lives. We talk sometimes about having children. Wouldn't you want to provide for them?"

"Yes. You're right again, of course. I love you and I

love the the life we have created. It's been a great trip so far and I just get caught up in the moment. My imagination gets the best of me. You know how it is."

Nadine reassures her husband with a firm hug. They relax in silence watching the waves. A few minutes pass and then a voice behind them speaks:

"Excuse me, I don't mean to interrupt, but I noticed that you aren't from around here and I wanted to welcome you to our humble little town."

Jonas and Nadine turn in unison to face the person speaking to them. They encounter an individual of striking appearance – a tall, well-built man with a deep tan and long blonde hair framing a chiseled face of classic proportions. The man's eyes are penetrating and startlingly blue. He wears a leather vest, leather pants, and leather moccasins, as if he stepped straight out of a storybook about Wild West pioneers. He gazes down upon Jonas and Nadine, intense and imposing.

"Would you care to join us by the fire?" the man asks. "Don't be shy. Nothing but good people around here."

Jonas looks at Nadine for direction. She smiles softly and shrugs. There is a look of concern in her eyes, though, Jonas notes.

"Yeah, okay," Jonas says, "but we can't stay long. "We're just passing through."

"That's what *everyone* says," the man laughs. "Ballena is a magical place. Most people find it difficult to leave once they've visited. If the town wants you to stay, you *stay*. I bet you were drawn here for a reason."

Jonas and Nadine follow the man to the fire. The musicians have started into a new song. No one pays any attention to the newcomers as they find an open spot and take a seat. The man in leather sits at Jonas' side. Those who aren't performing, including Jonas and Nadine, sit listening for the duration of the song. It seems to be an original number. The lyrics are thoughtful and poetic, the subject matter socially aware and strangely relevant. When the song is over, the air is heavy, the mood pensive. The man in leather speaks, breaking the thick silence: "I would like everyone to welcome our two new friends. I'm sorry, I didn't get your names."

"I'm Jonas, and this is Nadine."

"Wonderful, thank you. I'm Coyote Buck, and this is my family. Welcome to Ballena."

Around the fire, all eyes turn to the young couple. They are greeted with smiles and warm, sincere salutations.

"Thanks," Jonas says. "It's a nice town. We drove up from the city. It's great to get away and I can see why you like it here. It's so remote and peaceful."

"And hidden," Nadine interjects. "We had a hard time finding it at first. I thought we were going to get lost."

"That's the way we like it," says Coyote Buck. "We don't really *want* to be found. I'm glad that you two managed to make it here. It was meant to be. Do you smoke?"

Coyote Buck pulls a comically large marijuana cigarette from a leather pouch on his hip and offers it to the astonished couple.

"Is that *pot?*" Nadine cries. "I don't do that stuff. Thanks anyway."

"I haven't smoked since college," Jonas says. "I think I'll pass."

"Fair enough," says Coyote Buck as he puts the massive joint to his lips and lights it. He inhales deeply and passes it to a scruffy-looking guitar player to his left. "We grow our own, purely organic. We grow all our own food, too. If you stick around, you can join us for the feast."

"Oh, I don't know about that," Nadine says. "We should probably get going soon. There's more we want to see up the coast. We appreciate the offer, though, and your hospitality."

"What else *is* there to see?" Coyote Buck asks. "This is the jewel of California right here. It doesn't get any better than where you are right now. I mean that in both a physical and a spiritual sense. Be in the *Now*, man. Embrace the moment."

Raised eyebrows and rolled eyes betray Nadine's desire to hide her skepticism. Jonas nods politely and says, "I know where you're coming from, believe me. I've had similar feelings lately. Unfortunately, we have a home and jobs to get back to."

"Yes," Nadine says. "Reality awaits. It would be nice to escape society and live happily ever after in a commune somewhere, but this isn't the '60s anymore."

"What makes you say that?" asks Coyote Buck. "Where do you think you are? *When* do you thing you are?"

The others gathered around the fire are now listening to the conversation intently. Through the fog of marijuana smoke, 20 pairs of eyes watch the exchange eagerly, knowingly. The observers are accustomed to Coyote Buck's conversational style. It is both a spectator sport and a teaching tool, meant to entertain and enlighten. Jonas takes the bait and enters the fray: "I am, for better or for worse, a modern man in the modern world. I've got some stress in my life and there are times when I wish I could just walk away from the madness, but I'm a pretty happy guy, all things considered. In 2016, I see that as an accomplishment in itself. There are lots of people in this world who have it far worse."

Coyote Buck carefully processes Jonas' words before speaking:

"2016? Is that really *when* you think you are? What if I told you that time and space are an illusion, that the only thing that is real is your mind?"

"I can't rule that out," Jonas replies. "That could very well be true."

"Oh, please," Nadine scoffs. "It's getting a little too psychedelic around here. I'll tell you what's real: I have to be at work at 9 AM tomorrow morning, and if I'm not, I don't get paid. Jonas, too. I think it's time we hit the road."

"Ballena brought you here, to *us*," Coyote Buck states gravely. "The only way you're leaving is if it *wants* you to leave."

Nadine stands up. "Is that a threat?" she demands. "Are you trying to scare us?"

"Not a threat – the *truth*."

"Alright," says Jonas rising to his feet. "I think it *is* time for us to get going. It's been fun. Thank you for the music... and for the interesting conversation. If we start driving now, we can be –"

Jonas freezes mid-sentence. He has his cell phone in his hand and is staring at its screen in disbelief. "That can't be right," he mutters. "How can it be 6 PM already? We just had lunch."

"It's all *maya*, my friend," smiles Coyote Buck, "an illusion – persistent and all-encompassing, but simply illusion. You were meant to be here, with us, right now. Ballena has plans for you."

"I don't know if I should be flattered or freaked out," says Jonas.

"We just lost track of time," Nadine says as she joins Jonas at his side. "That's what happens when you're having fun. The sun is setting. Let's go."

The sky transforms into a magnificent display of warm reds and oranges as the ocean swallows the sun. Bands of clouds spread the color through the atmosphere. The rolling waves carry the shades to the shore in shimmering pulses of light. On the beach, the shadows elongate and distort. The day is quickly ebbing away.

Jonas and Nadine peel away from the group on the beach and head toward their parked car. Coyote Buck watches them, his face neutral, his eyes piercing them with laser intensity. The couple climbs the concrete steps that lead from the beach to the street. At the top, out of the sight of Coyote Buck and his followers, Nadine exhales sharply and shakes her head. "The sooner we get out of here, the better," she says. "This place is creepy."

"Yeah, I'm sorry about that. It's a really nice town in a beautiful area. Too bad the residents are all weirdos. At least the food..." Jonas freezes. "Oh, *shit!*"

"What is it?"

The couple has reached their car, but Jonas is mortified by what he sees. "A flat tire," he groans. "That's just *great.*"

"Oh, no, honey," says Nadine as she walks around the vehicle. "They're *all* flat."

"How the hell? The road coming in was rough, but not *that* rough. Someone must have done this."

"What are we going to do? I don't want to be stuck here all night."

"Let's just relax for a moment and breathe. Don't panic. I can call someone for help."

Jonas reaches into his pocket and retrieves his cell phone. When he sees the screen, he sighs. "No service. What a friggin' surprise."

"Really? What is wrong with this place? It's like a parallel reality. I just want to go home."

Jonas rubs his forehead, struggling to comprehend the situation and formulate a solution. "I'm at a loss for ideas," he says. "This is just insane. Maybe we should ask Elvis for help, or at least see if he has a phone we can use."

"The old guy at the restaurant? Do you think we can

trust him? What if it was him who did this?"

"I don't know if we can trust *anyone* around here, but what choice do we have? We only have one spare."

Reluctantly, Nadine follows Jonas back to the seafood restaurant where, in their perception of time, they had just finished eating. With no cars parked in front and no exterior lights, it appears to be closed for the evening. Jonas approaches the building anyway and tries to open the door. It is locked. He begins knocking forcefully.

"Hello? Are you in there, Elvis? It's Nadine and Jonas. We need help."

From behind the locked door, a voice calls out, firm and serious: "I told you to leave. I warned you about staying in town after dark. There's nothing I can do for you now. You're on your own."

Distressed, Nadine steps forward and bangs on the door with a clenched fist. "Please," she cries, "just let us use your phone. Our tires are flat and we have no way of getting out of here. We're trapped."

"Yes, I know," replies Elvis, his voice now expressing concern and a touch of sorrow. "You *are* trapped, dear. Both of you, like many before. Believe me, I would help if I could. I like you two – I really do – but the best thing for everyone right now is if you just step away from the door and make peace with your fate."

"What are you *talking* about?" yells Jonas. "Just let us use your phone! Or call someone *for* us – Triple A, the cops... *anyone!*"

"This is your last warning," Elvis says. "Get away from here. I have a gun and will defend myself if need be." The sound of a shotgun being cocked accompanies the last statement, as if reinforcing the point.

"This whole town is nuts," Nadine says, stepping away from the restaurant. Tears are forming in her eyes. She is on the verge of hysteria. Jonas notices her building anxiety and wraps an arm around her.

"The only thing I can think of is to go back to the beach," Jonas says. "Surely *someone* will help us. They can't *all* be psychos like that Coyote character."

"What if it was one of them who did this to us?"

"Then we'll confront them. I really don't think it *was* one of them, though. They're too busy getting high and playing hippie on the beach. It was probably just a couple of local kids who noticed an unfamiliar car and wanted to play a practical joke on some tourists – a pain in the ass, but nothing sinister."

"Have you even *seen* any kids around here? It's like a ghost town except for the freaks, stoners, and surfers."

"What are our options? We have no choice but to ask for help. Don't let your imagination get the best of you. We're going to be fine. We'll be back at home before you know it."

"That's all I want now – just to be back at the house, safe and comfortable. I think I've had enough adventure for one day."

Jonas and Nadine walk back toward the beach as the sun slips fully below the horizon. They reach the steps and descend. The glow of the fire pit illuminates the gathering, which seems to have grown in size. The festive atmosphere has intensified. The mood is wild and raucous. As the attendees imbibe, ingest, and indulge, a full moon hangs overhead like a celestial lantern – or a giant eye, sentient and omniscient.

Spotting Coyote Buck sitting in the same position by the fire as before, Jonas and Nadine approach. Coyote Buck smiles when he sees them. He gives them a friendly wave and encourages them to join him with a hand gesture.

"I knew you'd be back," Coyote Buck says. "I told you – you belong here. Ballena has plans for you."

"Actually, we ran into a problem," says Jonas. "We somehow ended up with four flat tires. Not one – *four.* So, as you can imagine, it's going to be a little hard for us to get home."

"You wouldn't happen to know anything about that, would you?" Nadine asks, her tone accusatory.

"Of course not," Coyote Buck replies. "I've been here the entire time. I haven't left the beach all day, nor has anyone else, as far as I know. We're having too good a time to do something mean and stupid like that."

Trying to diffuse the tension, Jonas waves his hands and says, "I know. We didn't really think it was you guys. We could have run over some glass on the way in, or something like that. We just need some help."

"I'll tell you what *I* think," says Coyote Buck. "It was synchronicity that brought you here and synchronicity that is keeping you. This is a special occasion, you know. We don't celebrate like this every night."

"*That's* a surprise," Nadine chuckles. "Do you people have jobs? We do, and they require us to be there tomorrow morning."

"I find it astonishing how people embrace their servitude," Coyote Buck says. "It's like the masses are totally cut off from Source and they don't even know it. The world would be a healthier and happier place if there was a return to natural law."

Three young women with similar long, straight, flowing hair and vintage '60s sundresses appear behind Jonas and Nadine. The women are smiling widely. Their faces radiate joy, but their limbs are rigid and their posture stiff. They stand in a tight line behind Jonas and Nadine, a little too close for comfort. The tallest one, a dark-haired girl in her early twenties, speaks: "It's almost time to begin the ceremony. The preparations are complete."

"Thank you, Susan," Coyote Buck smiles. "You and the girls did a fabulous job this year. Have you met the guests of honor yet? This is Jonas and Nadine."

"Hello," says Susan, her eyes eerily vacant. "I'm so glad you could join us."

"Guests of honor," Nadine scoffs. "Hardly. This really isn't our kind of party."

"We'll be leaving as soon as we get our car fixed," says Jonas.

"You keep saying that," Coyote Buck says, "yet here you are. Unlike the sad fools who wander the city like zombies, blind to the truth and deaf to the inner voices of their hearts, *I* have a connection with Source. The ocean speaks to me. That's why I'm here... and that's also why *you're* here."

Coyote Buck nods at Susan, who is still standing behind Jonas and Nadine. "It's time," he says softly, gravely. Instantly, the three girls spring into action. With frightening speed and uncanny strength, Coyote Buck's female minions immobilize Jonas and Nadine in a coordinated attack. In a flash they have pinned the arms of the shocked couple behind their backs. Before Jonas and Nadine have time to process what is happening, Susan expertly binds their wrists with thick rope.

When the other beach revelers realize what is happening, a hush descends upon the group. The laughter and music cease. All eyes fixate on Coyote Buck and Jonas and Nadine, who are now bound and restrained by a small group of Coyote Buck's followers.

"It's best if you don't fight," Coyote Buck states. "Trust in the wisdom of the cosmos and embrace your fate."

"Why are you doing this?" Nadine cries.

Nadine writhes and struggles, but she and her husband are held firmly by people who are determined to make sure that they do not escape. Jonas remains still and, for the moment, silent. The situation had escalated so quickly that he has not yet fully grasped the gravity of their predicament.

"It's nothing personal," says Coyote Buck. "As head of this family, I need to do what is best for us, and occasionally, that means I have to make hard decisions for the greater good. This is not something I enjoy doing, and I apologize for the rough handling. When we meet on the other side, I hope you are able to forgive me and know that all exists in harmony. This is simply part of the balance of karma."

Jonas, coming to terms with their situation, now speaks up. With great effort, he maintains his cool in an attempt to reason with Coyote Buck. "You are making a huge mistake. Whatever it is you're planning to do, you won't get away with it. Too many witnesses. Do you trust all of these people to keep a secret? Look around you. I understand that you want to keep this town private. Why don't you just let us go? Nobody ever has to know we were here. We won't say a thing. No one even needs to know this place exists."

"I'm glad you understand our desire to keep Ballena private," Coyote Buck says. "We live here in peace and prosperity because the land and the ocean take care of us. In return, we take care of the land and the ocean."

Coyote Buck gazes out upon the ocean, vast and deep, sparkling ethereally in reflected moonlight. Concealed within its immense depths is an expansive, hidden world full of mysterious structures and strange life forms – an alien ecosystem surrounding our own.

Susan, who appears to be Coyote Buck's most trusted accomplice, speaks up: "It's almost time. I can feel Him coming."

"Yes," says Coyote Buck. "I feel Him too. He's

calling out to us. I can hear His voice in my head. Bring the offerings to the water's edge. Bind their legs and seal their mouths. I don't want a repeat of last year's ceremony, which was messy, loud, and disturbing for the new followers. Let's do it right this year."

Coyote Buck reaches into the leather pouch at his side and produces a six-shot revolver. He hands the gun to Susan. "Take this. Use it if you need to, but only to wound. The offerings must remain alive."

"Please don't do this!" screams Nadine as one of the men restraining her produces a roll of duct tape. "We won't tell anyone. Let us go!"

The man ignores Nadine's cries and seals her mouth with the tape. Jonas' mouth is also sealed. They are led away from Coyote Buck by Susan and the two silent girls and directed toward the water. Before they reach the shoreline, an extraordinary event occurs, accompanied by shrieks of delight and excited cheering from the onlookers on the beach.

"He's here!" Susan cries.

500 or so yards out from the beach, a frothy, churning maelstrom forms on the surface of the ocean. Massive fountains of water shoot into the air and cascade back down like raging geysers. The tempest builds, violent and awesome, increasing in size and fury. Something is coming to the surface – something enormous and unimaginably powerful. When the indistinct, gargantuan shape breaches the surface, it unleashes a deafening roar that seems to shake the fabric of reality. The sound reverberates like the war cry of a demented demon. A tentacle rises from the beast, uncoiling and stretching 100 feet in the air before crashing down with an ear-splitting slap and an explosion of water.

"Yes, He's here," Coyote Buck calls from a safe distance away, "and He's hungry."

With the gun in her hand, Susan urges the bound

couple forward. Rough handling by the two other girls ensure that they comply. When they reach the edge of the shore, with water lapping at their feet, Jonas and Nadine are forced to their knees. Out of the ocean, the great monstrosity churns up water and produces a great wake as it speeds toward them. Somehow, it seems to know that two delicious morsels await.

Nadine struggles against her bindings. She topples over on her side and something pops out of the front pocket of her jeans. Susan, who is still standing behind her, gasps when she sees the object – it is the ceramic dragon that Jonas had purchased for Nadine the day before they left on their journey. Susan bends down and plucks it out of the sand.

"Buck," Susan shouts. "You better come see this."

Coyote Buck curses and yells, "What the hell is going on? He's coming! Leave them and get the fuck out of there!"

"You *really* need to see this," Susan reiterates.

"Goddamn," Coyote Buck mutters, "this better be good." He marches up the beach and approaches Susan, who is holding the tiny dragon in the palm of her hand. He freezes when he sees it. "Is that what I think it is?" he asks.

"It's a dragon," Susan nods. "Just like in your dream."

"Well, isn't *that* interesting."

"What does it mean?"

"It means that we need to reconsider our plans for the evening. Help them up and untie them."

"What about Him?" Susan gestures toward the massive shape racing toward the shore.

"*When the dragon appears, the beast will be defeated.* That's what the dream said. I'm not sure exactly what that means, but I think we're about to find out."

Susan and the henchmen help Jonas and Nadine to their feet. They release the rope bindings and remove the tape from their mouths.

Jonas gasps for air and speaks, "That thing out there

might be an actual sea monster, or I may be hallucinating, but I know this: You people are *nuts*."

"You have no idea what's going on," Coyote Buck says. "There is a larger reality that totally eludes the mundane minds of modern men. You should just be thankful that you didn't end up in the gut of that incredible animal. It is more ancient, powerful, and wise than you can possibly imagine."

"What happens now?" asks Susan. "Do we just let them go? Doesn't the beast need to feed?"

"They can go," replies Coyote Buck as he gazes out on the sea. "A new age is dawning."

"Can I have my dragon back?" Nadine asks. "It has special meaning to me."

"Take it," Says Coyote Buck. "Leave now."

Susan places the dragon in Nadine's hand. Nadine and Jonas walk up the beach away from the shore. The crowd gathered around the fire pit watches the couple pass in reverent silence. When they reach the concrete steps that will take them up to the street, Jonas turns around once more to look at the ocean. He sees the leviathan, its unfathomably large shape moving toward the shore, tentacles thrashing and water raging. Coyote and his closest followers still stand on the beach awaiting its arrival, their forms dwarfed by the ancient behemoth.

"I'm ready to go home," Jonas says.

"What about the car?" says Nadine.

"We'll figure something out. We always do. It's funny – the city suddenly seems not so bad. Who'd have thought I'd actually be looking forward to getting back to the chaos and confusion?"

"In a week, you'll be wanting to go on another adventure. I know you."

Jonas and Nadine walk hand-in-hand toward their car. Behind them, the beast bellows, its great roar shaking the foundations of the surrounding buildings and rattling windows. Jonas and Nadine shudder and draw closer together. They do not look back.

Dream Sequence

1

At precisely 8:15 AM, the skybus arrived at the boarding station. A young man named Miles was among the small group of people who waited atop the fenced and gated platform that towered 100 feet above the ground. Miles was just beginning his daily routine, the initial stage of which consisted of a rather long commute to the city center, where he correlated data at a large research facility. Unlike the others around him, Miles was not fully engrossed by the inner screen of an E-Visor. His device had recently malfunctioned and he felt anxious, exposed, and awkward without it. He watched the skybus approach with naked, jittery eyes as he clutched his bagged lunch tightly to his chest.

The autonomous skybus slid into place in front of the platform. Miles and the other commuters walked up to the turnstile and, one at a time, they waved their implanted hands over the embedded sensor. A green light and a bright tone indicated a successful transaction and allowed admittance. The passengers filed on in a smooth, efficient, robotic procession. Miles was the last one to board. As he habitually did every morning, he went directly to the seat in the right rear of the vehicle and sat down. The other regular riders also sat in their usual seats, as if predestined or programmed. The door slid shut and the skybus quietly pulled away from the platform at a high rate of speed.

Miles leaned against the wall of the skybus and gazed down at the sprawling metropolis below him. He sighed.

Another day in the machine, he thought. *Another work cycle crunching numbers for the Bot, and now I don't even have a visor to kill time with. God, it's all so dreary and endless...*

Boredom and an intense weariness fell upon Miles. The awful, infinite ennui settled into his bones and seemed to add actual mass to his body, which hung on his spirit like rotten meat on a strained rack. Miles shifted his gaze forward. A few rows in front of him sat a young couple. They were apparently together, but each was clearly mesmerized by whatever application their E-Visors were running. Their slack, immobile frames mirrored Miles', but he had the unfortunate disadvantage of being fully aware of the brutal banality of his existence. Miles studied the backs of their heads and wondered: *Are they happy? Are they enjoying this ridiculous charade called Life? At least they have each other. It would be nice to have someone. I wish I were unconscious. I wish I had my visor.* Another long, drawn-out sigh escaped his lips, carrying with it the medicinal smell of his morning's rations.

Sudden movement, quick and flitting, caught Miles' attention. He looked to his left and gasped. He could see, through the side window, three large, transparent orbs flying toward the skybus. The orbs were piloted by helmeted men and they were rushing at him *fast.* Miles was startled to see, protruding from each orb and aimed directly at the skybus, several extremely menacing and obviously lethal weapons. They extended from the front of each orb like insect stingers.

Miles jumped up and called out, "Help! Help! We're being attacked!" No one seemed to hear him. The other passengers were entirely unaware of what was occurring just outside the vehicle. The orbs were closing in. Miles became frantic. He ran up the aisle and reached out to the closest person, a man in a seat a few rows up on the left side. The man was chuckling to himself, obviously enjoying whatever he was viewing on the inner screen of his visor. Miles grasped the man's shoulder with a firm grip and shook him. "Hey! Hey!" he shouted. "We're in serious trouble! Look out the window!" The man in the seat did not respond – he simply giggled, completely immersed in his media.

"Someone listen to me!" Miles panicked. A glance over his shoulder revealed that the orbs were now mere yards away from the skybus. Miles could see the skybus' reflection in the black glass of the closest orb pilot's helmet. Miles ran up to the couple he had been staring at only minutes before. "Hey, you two!" he cried. "Wake up! Wake up!" The young man and woman remained slumped in their seats, unconscious. For a brief moment Miles wondered if they were dead, but he quickly realized the truth. "Stupid digital drugs," he muttered.

It was too late anyway. Miles turned to face the window just in time to see the orbs zoom up to the skybus, stop suddenly in mid-flight, and open fire as they hovered. Blasts of bright plasma pulsed from the energy weapons and tore through the skybus. Before he and the other passengers were engulfed and incinerated in the deadly salvo, a peculiar thought entered Miles' head: *This has already happened to me. I dreamed this.*

2

"Target neutralized. Returning with squad to HQ." The orb pilot addressed his commander through his neural mesh interface as he pulled up from the flaming debris of the falling skybus. His two wingmen assumed their positions at his flanks and the small formation sped away on a northeastern trajectory. They had only traveled a few hundred feet when the commander issued new orders to the squad leader. The voice was internal – loud and clear in the pilot's head, distinct from his own thoughts: "We have a developing situation and we need you on the scene. Go directly to the provided coordinates. Engage protocol for civil unrest."

A series of numbers were transmitted directly into the squad leader's mind and he fed them into the orb's guidance system, which was linked to those of his wingmen. The three orbs changed course and flew toward the location in perfect synchronization. They were in transit for only a few minutes before the chaotic scene became visible just ahead. A crowd of demonstrators numbering in the hundreds had gathered in front of an administrative building. They were carrying hand-painted signs and crude weapons fashioned from sharpened sticks and agricultural implements. The fearsome, unruly mass of men and women were yelling and chanting, primal and livid.

"HQ, we have visual contact," said the squad leader. "We have an unlawful congregation of civilians. They appear to be gathered in protest."

"Disperse the crowd with appropriate force," the commander ordered. "25% casualty rate is ideal, 50% is acceptable."

"Roger that."

The orb pilot activated his weapon and pulled ahead of his small squad. When he was a few yards away from the mob, he dived in and opened fire. His wingmen followed his lead. Brilliant blasts of plasma tore into the crowd. People scattered in panic. Some were killed instantly and fell in smoking heaps of charred flesh. Others bravely, defiantly, futilely threw sticks, rakes, and shovels at the orbs. The useless weapons bounced off the thick, tempered glass and clattered to the ground. After their initial sweep, the orbs turned around and flew back for another pass, unleashing a second burst at the terrified and disorganized crowd. More people fell victim to the deadly barrage tearing through their ranks.

"The situation is under control," said the orb pilot. "Requesting permission to return to HQ."

"Engage the targets once more," the commander responded. "This has been happening too frequently. We need to send these savages a message."

The pilot swung his craft around in a wide arc. The crowd below him had thinned considerably. Most of those who had not been killed had fled. Only a small, tightly-packed core group of demonstrators remained in front of the administrative building. In the face of death, they obstinately stood their ground, waving their implements and chanting in unison. The orb pilot flew directly toward them, ready to release hellfire. Just as he was about to squeeze the trigger, the pilot caught a glimpse of a man in the crowd with a metallic object in his hand. The man was snarling and looking directly at the approaching orb. Before the pilot could react, the man launched the object, which struck the craft just above the protruding weapon and exploded on contact. The fireball blinded the pilot. The pilot lost control and the orb suddenly careened down and to the right. He struggled to pull up, but quickly realized it was to no avail. A crash was inevitable.

"I've been hit," the pilot announced to his superiors. "An explosive device of unknown type. I'm going down."

As the orb tumbled out of the sky, racing, erratic thoughts filled the pilot's head: *How did they get real weapons? Am I going to die? Melanie, I love you.* The craft hit the ground. The glass shattered and the pilot was thrown from the vehicle. He landed hard on the pavement, fracturing his skull, breaking multiple bones, and rupturing organs. Through the fog of agony, the pilot could see the surviving demonstrators rushing at him. They descended on him, shouting, swinging, beating, and tearing.

3

They're going to kill him, Stella realized as she watched the mob attack the fallen orb pilot. *I can't watch this.*

Yet Stella did watch. Though horrified, she was mesmerized by the brutality on display before her. She had never seen her friends and compatriots behave in such a primitive, ferocious way. They were screaming as they assailed the helpless man on the ground – it was the shriek of a demented hive-mind. The pilot made feeble attempts to defend himself from the blows that rained down upon him and the rabid, vicious, ripping hands that clawed at his tattered uniform. He was weakening quickly. The crowd sensed his wavering strength and intensified their assault. In a whirlwind of violence, the mob stripped the pilot and beat him unconscious. They continued the attack until the pilot was a bloody, broken, misshapen heap. With a final roar, one of the young men in the mob raised a baseball bat high over his head and brought it down on the pilot's head. As the bat struck, it made a wet crunch and it was obvious that the pilot was now truly, and very, dead.

Above the carnage and destruction, the remaining two orbs in the squad continued to circle. Inexplicably, they were not firing at the surviving demonstrators. Stella watched as they made one final pass before accelerating and shooting off. In a blink, they were gone. The courtyard in front of the administrative building now looked like a combat zone. Bodies and debris covered the entire plaza. Stella had expected violence, but she had not been prepared for the intensity of what she had just experienced. In a sudden rush of emotion, she dropped to her knees and began to weep loudly.

"Stella!" cried her friend Adam, rushing to her side. "Are you okay?"

Adam knelt down and wrapped an arm around Stella's quivering body. "Hey, don't cry," he said. "We got one of those bastards! We should be celebrating!"

"We're no better than they are," Stella sobbed. "We're all just a bunch of animals."

"This is a revolution, Stella. Blood will be shed. I am very proud of our brothers and sisters who lost their lives today in the fight against tyranny. This was a victory for our side, don't you see that?"

"We all could have been killed. I don't know why we weren't. Those orbs could have wiped us out. Why did they retreat?"

Stella began to regain her composure. She stood up and shook off Adam's consoling arm. She looked around, absorbing the details of the chaos around her. Some survivors were tending to the wounded, others were checking the dead. Some sat or stood with blank expressions on their faces, traumatized by the event. A few smiled and chatted excitedly, clearly elated and thoroughly enjoying themselves. As Stella took it all in, a loud, shrill siren pierced the air. Above them now, where the orbs had launched their deadly attack minutes before, a large, cylindrical drone hovered. Bright blue and red lights rotated around its perimeter. From an on-board speaker, a robotic voice announced: "This area is now closed to civilians. Move out immediately. Failure to comply will result in lethal force."

"We need to get out of here *now*," Adam insisted. "The orbs are bad, but the drones are much, much worse. I've seen them level entire city blocks."

A tall, bearded man wearing a black jacket with obscure insignia on its shoulders addressed the group: "Excellent work, everyone. Let's gather the dead and wounded and get out of here. We'll plan our next move at the compound."

The demonstrators sprung into action. The man in the black jacket was their clear leader and he had their unanimous respect and obedience.

"I'm starting to wonder if these protests are doing any good at all," Stella said, mostly to herself. "Are we making progress? We've been losing so many people lately."

"Of course we're making progress!" cried Adam. "We actually destroyed one of their orbs today! That's huge. Do you know how many millions of dollars one of those things costs?"

"I lost friends today. So did you. How much were their lives worth?"

"We gain new recruits daily. Our numbers are growing. The tide is turning in our favor. Come on, now – let's get the fuck out of here before we get nuked."

Stella and Adam joined the others. In a long, slow procession, the group moved out of the courtyard and into the street. The drone hovered in its position high above the plaza, its lights still flashing, its siren still screeching. The battered and bloody column of dissenters, led by the man in the black jacket, made its way through the labyrinthine downtown streets. They marched, the dead and wounded carried by the living and fit, under the blazing, midsummer sun, which cast a harsh, sandy yellow light on the metal and concrete guts of the city. The occupants of the few vehicles that the group encountered ignored the procession.

The column marched until it reached a highway overpass. It crossed over the abandoned freeway and, once on the other side, worked its way down the embankment and under the overpass. Concealed below the structure was the entrance to a hidden tunnel, covered with a camouflaged gate. The gate was opened and the group entered. The tunnel was narrow and unlit. Its width only allowed the procession to traverse it two abreast. Warm, rank, ankle-high fluid flowed through the tunnel. The thin column snaked forward, sloshing through the darkness.

After an hour's march through the dank underworld, light appeared at the end of the tunnel – a faint, flickering glow that grew brighter as the group approached, reaching toward them like a sentient tendril of illumination. The light emanated from a chamber. The group, exhausted, wet, filthy, and near-delirious, reached the entrance and filed through.

The chamber was spacious and rectangular – essentially a large, underground concrete box. It served as the headquarters and home of the primary anti-establishment organization in the region. They went by the name of S.U.R.G.E. and they had occupied this location for over a year. On the left side of the chamber, blankets, sleeping bags, pillows, and clothes were spread over the floor haphazardly. This was where the group slept, and it was where they now sought rest. Before the wounded and weary laid down their heads, the dead were carefully arranged along a far wall and covered with sheets. The somber ritual was conducted silently and meticulously by people who had done the same thing many times before.

"Will this war ever end?" Stella sighed as she collapsed on a dirty pile of blankets in the corner. "My father used to tell me stories of his childhood, when peace still existed in most parts of the world. Seems like a fantasy, doesn't it?"

"That's dangerous thinking, Stella," Adam said. "We must always keep our hearts and minds focused on the goal."

"Which is what, exactly?"

"I hope you're joking. Do I really have to remind you what we're doing, what our comrades have sacrificed their lives for?"

"I'm just tired. I feel drained."

"I need you to stay strong, Stella. *We* need you to stay

strong. Trust our leadership. They have a view of the larger perspective. They will not let us down."

"All I've ever known is death, destruction, misery. At least the non-resistors have safe, predictable, *stable* lives."

"Is that what you want? You joined the rebellion when I did, and for the same reasons. Get your fucking head together and remember why we're here. We must *never* give up. We must *never* waver. We *must* persist in this struggle until we have overthrown the tyrannical regime of the oligarchs. The cause is more important than you, me, or any other individual – alive or dead – in this room. Do you understand?"

"You sound like *him*." Stella gestured with her head toward the man in the black jacket, who was sitting separate from the group and examining papers.

"Nothing wrong with that," Adam smiled. "He's a great man and I'm proud to serve him. Perhaps *you* should try to emulate him a little more."

"I've been fighting just as long and just as hard as you, Adam. You know that. I'm just starting to get a weird... *feeling*. It's almost like there isn't supposed to be a winner in this conflict. It's like the hate and carnage *is* the point of the war. It's hard to explain."

Stella turned over on her side, facing away from Adam, who sat cross-legged, sharpening a large hunting knife. "I miss my family," she said quietly. "I miss cats and babies and music. I miss joy. I miss laughing."

Adam chuckled and said, "Sounds nice, but let's be honest – that stuff is just a sentimental daydream. I actually like fighting. Makes me feel *alive*. You used to be a vicious warrior – a stone-cold *killer* – what happened to you?"

"I feel like I'm waking up from a nightmare."

4

Hidden in the shadows of the tunnel, a crouched figure watched the column of resistors march toward their secret headquarters below the city streets. When the last of them had passed, the figure stealthily emerged from a hiding place against the wall and began creeping out the way the column had come. Slinking, sneaking, edging its way out, the figure moved like a serpentine humanoid. It reached the entrance to the tunnel and stepped out into the cool, golden dusk. It scanned its surroundings and, satisfied that all was clear, relaxed its posture. It climbed the embankment and walked though the fading light toward the city center.

Before the Escalation, this strange, timid, feral creature had a name and an identity, just like every other person in the city that they had all called home. The creature's name occasionally returned in dreams – *Cameron* – but it had lost its meaning. Cameron was once a happy, normal, loving and loved little boy, but after his parents were killed in the uprising eight years ago, he had fled the city. The tunnels were now Cameron's home and survival had become all he knew.

Cameron walked along the side of the highway, staying close to the bushes, ready to duck for cover at the first sign of potential trouble. His senses were keen and his reflexes sharp. Tattered remnants of scavenged clothing hung on his gaunt frame. His hair was bushy and wild, his eyes piercing and alert. A nascent beard was just beginning to darken his jawline. He was 13 years old, but he had seen and experienced more suffering and horror than most will in a lifetime.

Just ahead now, a few hundred feet away, was the exit that led into the city center. Cameron paused and scanned his surroundings intently, his eyes wide, probing for even the slightest movement in the growing dark. His acute hearing was fully tuned to his environment, sensitive to the quietest of sounds. Cameron tilted his head back and took a few deep sniffs. Sensing no danger, he crept toward the turn-off. Staying on the shoulder of the road, he approached the exit, which branched off to the right. He stayed low and scurried down the embankment.

Like a rodent in the forest, Cameron made his way through the city, sticking to the dead neighborhoods and alleyways when possible. He bolted from shadow to shadow, nerves taut and vibrating, his head an electric sentinel of total awareness. Finally, he arrived at his destination – a small diner in the heart of the city. The sight of the overflowing dumpster at the back of the building made his stomach growl. Cameron grunted and sprinted toward it. With one hand, he held the lid open and with the other, he began rooting through the rancid-smelling contents. He was delighted to find a delectable treat – a nearly whole mold-free hamburger. He squealed happily and jammed the dripping burger into his mouth. He gobbled it up in moments and resumed his search.

"Hey! Don't you fucking move!" cried a voice from behind him. Cameron spun around in shock. He had let his guard down and had not sensed the approaching person. Standing before Cameron now was a large man in a stained, white smock. The man blocked the exit out of the alley. He was holding a large assault rifle that was aimed directly at Cameron. Cameron realized instantly that he was trapped and in mortal danger.

"So you're the one who keeps digging through my garbage," the man said. "I thought it was freakin' raccoons. Do you know what kind of mess you've been making? I oughta blow your head off and dump your body in with them rotten burgers you like so much."

Cameron was frozen in abject fear. Only his eyes

moved – they darted about looking for an escape. The man with the gun looked through the sights of the weapon and said, "Ain't you got anything to say, boy? What's wrong with you? You slow in the head?" When understanding dawned on the armed man – that the frightened boy who quivered before him was perhaps not slow in the head, but was certainly not *right* – he lowered his weapon and sighed. "Where'd you come from, boy? Where's your family?"

Cameron's eyes dropped to the ground and his body slackened.

"They dead, ain't they?" said the man. "Well, shit. Lots of that going on. It's a sad state of affairs when kids have to live on the street 'cause their parents got killed. I'm sorry, boy. I've lost a lot of people, too. It hurts."

Though he remained silent, Cameron's eyes watered up. He had long ago compartmentalized the memories of his parents, but they returned with an emotional punch at the mere mention of them. In an instant, he reverted back to the vulnerable and scared state of a toddler who has just lost the most important people in his life. The shock and distress was made all the worse by the fact that Cameron had actually witnessed it happen.

"Mommy," Cameron whimpered. "Daddy."

The man from the restaurant slowly approached and gently wrapped an arm around Cameron's shoulders. "Hey, little buddy," he said, "it's alright. Don't cry. Are you hungry? Why don't you come in with me? I'll make you a fresh burger. It'll taste better than the slimy, wormy ones you've been diggin' out of this bin! Trust me. Fries, too... How does that sound?"

The sensation of the man's arm around him – warm and strong and safe – was both alien and familiar to Cameron. It caused him first to tense up, then to immediately relax and melt into the comforting embrace. Cameron allowed himself to be led out of the alley, around to the front, and into the building.

"Welcome to Fat Rob's," the man said. "And, yes, I'm Fat Rob. I was just closing up, but I can get the grill going again and make you one of my world-famous greasy masterpieces. Have a seat."

Fat Rob directed Cameron to the front of the empty diner. Cameron was beginning to warm up to the big man. He hopped up on a stool at the counter and playfully twisted in his seat a few times. A small smile appeared on his face. It felt good to be indoors. It felt good to be in the presence of another human. It felt good to let his guard down. Cameron wanted so badly to trust someone, *anyone*. He knew that Fat Rob could have gunned him down in the alley and disposed of his body without anyone ever knowing. Instead, he had invited him into this warm and comfortable place – a place where normal people ate and talked and laughed.

Fat Rob went to his grill. "You're gonna love this, boy," he said. "Let's put some meat on those bones."

As Fat Rob prepared the grill, a thunderous explosion in the street outside the diner rocked the entire building, blowing out the front window and door in a cloud of glass and wood. Cameron's animal instincts immediately returned and he leaped off the stool to take cover behind the counter. Fat Rob dropped, too, with a loud shout. "Fuck!" he cried. "Not again. Stay down, boy. We're in for some trouble."

Fat Rob reached over. Without exposing himself, he retrieved his assault rifle from where he had left it leaning against the wall by the grill. "These pieces of shit aren't getting away with it this time," he snarled. "I'm ready for 'em."

There was another bang, and the door to the diner was kicked open. Through the smoke and dust stepped a technological and biological monstrosity – a lumbering, menacing, rampaging hybrid of man and machine. It was mostly robotic – a metallic, humanoid frame of highly advanced alloys interlaced with cutting-edge circuitry – but attached to its broad and fearsome shoulders was the head of a man. The head was flesh and bone, but the brain was interlaced with the same circuitry as the robotic body. The eyes of the monstrosity blazed with malevolence as it crashed through the entrance. Following directly behind it was another hybrid, equally frightful in appearance. The destructive potential of the beasts was obvious.

"Rogues," whispered Fat Rob. "Defectors from the force... or maybe just defective. This is the third time this year they've robbed me. I swear, I'm not going to let it happen again. Stay down, boy, if you don't want to get hurt."

The two hybrids stomped their way into the diner, their massive, metal feet pulverizing glass and wood with each heavy step. They stopped in the center of the room. "I see you!" called the first, its voice gleefully human. "Why don't you come on out. We have business to discuss."

Still crouched behind the counter, with Cameron cowering at his side, Fat Rob gritted his teeth and steeled himself. He had no intention of discussing business – or anything else, for that matter. He inhaled deeply and sprung into action. In a flurry of motion – a surprising flurry for a man of his size, Fat Rob jumped to his feet and expertly brought his weapon into firing position. He pulled the trigger and unleashed a barrage of military-grade hollow-points at the first hybrid. The hybrid's head vaporized in pink mist and its robotic frame crashed to the floor. Fat Rob quickly aimed his weapon at the second hybrid, which had drawn its own weapon: a mini-cannon mounted to its forearm. The ominous barrel of the cannon was trained on Rob. It would no doubt reduce the man to a smoking pile of gelatinous matter in a microsecond. Fat Rob bravely held his ground, his rifle steadfastly fixed on the hybrid.

"Classic standoff," Fat Rob remarked. "I bet you didn't see that coming. Maybe you assholes weren't aware of the fact that I served two tours in the war. I've blown away many, many of you rusty abominations. Glad to have the chance to do it again."

The hybrid stared at Fat Rob with a blank expression on its face. For a pregnant, tense moment, the room was still and silent.

Without lowering its deadly hand-cannon, the hybrid finally spoke: "Where did you get that weapon?" It asked the question with genuine curiosity.

"Yeah, I thought you might like it," Rob replied. "See, I wasn't dumb enough to give up my arms when they made their sweeps. I knew I'd need a little protection from scum like you. I've got a lot more, in fact, hidden away. They're antiques now, but I keep them clean and in good working order, as you've just seen."

"I should blow you and this whole place away," the hybrid said. "It stinks in here. You bios disgust me. I can see your little friend hiding behind the counter. His heat signature is clearer than yours."

"So why don't you?" Rob asked.

"Believe it or not, I've got a soft spot for the young ones."

The hybrid lowered its arm and the attached cannon. It glanced down at its fallen partner and sighed. "This unit was worth more than you and all the other meatbags in this entire neighborhood combined."

"Nothing but scrap metal now," Rob smiled, his weapon still aimed at the hybrid's head. "Why don't you just leave it for me to clean up? I might even make enough selling spare parts to pay for the damages you fucks caused."

"This isn't over. You haven't seen the last of me."

"So be it. I need more friends in my life anyway."

The hybrid pivoted and started toward the entrance. It walked over the debris piled at the threshold and stepped out into the night. Fat Rob watched it through the shattered window as it marched up the street. When the hybrid was out of sight, Fat Rob lowered his rifle.

"It's gone," Rob said. "You can come out now, boy."

Cameron sat with his legs drawn up to his chest. He was trembling and breathing rapidly and erratically. Fat Rob knelt down and put his hands on Cameron's shoulders. He looked him in the eye and said, "Everything's okay. We're safe, at least for now. I won't let anyone or anything hurt you, do you understand? You can stay with me for as long as you want. Would you like that?"

Cameron's breathing relaxed somewhat. In a small, shaky voice, he said, "Yes. Want to stay with you."

"Alright then! That's good. I want you to stay, too. We've got some cleaning to do, and some of it isn't going to be pleasant. Can you handle that?"

Cameron gently nodded.

"Good boy. Why don't we get some grub in our guts first? Before we were so rudely interrupted, I was about to whip up one of my greasy masterpieces. Blasting hybrids always makes me hungry. Let's eat!"

5

The hybrid walked the dark, empty streets in search of a fix. The attempted robbery of the diner had not gone as planned. With no currency, and its partner in crime dead and disabled at the hands of the unusually resilient and unexpectedly armed fat proprietor of the restaurant, the hybrid considered its options. The early evening dose of Tonik was beginning to wear off. Soon the highly unpleasant withdrawal symptoms would appear. If the hybrid did not find a connection soon, an agonizing, searing pain would fill its skull like spinning blades of red-hot steel. Not long after that, the hybrid would begin to lose motor control. Its brain would cease to communicate with its robotic body and it would be left immobile and powerless, a useless pile of mechanical and electrical components. Then, disconnected from its life support, the head would quickly die. It was a scenario that the hybrid planned to avoid at all costs.

The hybrid scanned the streets with its augmented vision as it prowled the nearly deserted inner city core. Here and there, it spotted the forms of lost, damaged, pathetic souls hiding among the rubble and filth of the dilapidated structures. Many, like the boy in the diner, were children. Somehow, through all the combat, horror, and programming that the hybrid had experienced, it still maintained sympathy for the young wretches. The sight of them always caused a distant, yet palpable, stirring of emotion in the buried remnants of the hybrid's humanity.

On this particular evening, all of the usual spots where the hybrid sought dealers – the shadowy alleys, hidden alcoves, and abandoned buildings – were deserted. The hybrid wondered if there had been a recent cleanup by the force, or perhaps even by citizen vigilantes. He had been seeing more and more illegal weaponry lately and, like the owner of the diner, more people willing to put up a fight. Things had changed in the last few years. The vice-like grip that the hybrids once had on the criminal underground was slackening noticeably.

A nauseous throbbing sensation was beginning to creep up the back of the hybrid's head, pulsing from deep within its brain. It was critical now – the hybrid needed the drug. It suddenly remembered that, not far from its current location, in a secret basement beneath a demolished office building, there was a 24-hour pleasure den. The hybrid had once sold harvested organs to the owner of the sordid establishment and had been paid well. He knew there would be plenty of Tonik there, along with other substances and contraband of every possible variety. It was not a place where the average street person or junkie could just show up, but hybrids were given special privileges. Most people, even the kings and queens of the crime syndicates, found them to be extremely volatile and often extraordinarily dangerous. The hybrids had the grudging respect of the underworld.

The hybrid picked up its pace and headed in the direction of the pleasure den. The pistons in its legs pumped in time with the escalating throbbing in its brain. It broke into a full-on run and covered the last few blocks in seconds. As it came to the destroyed office complex, a drone patrolling above cast a moving spotlight on the ground below. Was it the Force? Did it belong to the Syndicate? The hybrid couldn't be sure – the law and the underworld often used the same equipment. In fact, the law and the underworld were often the same people.

The hybrid was getting desperate and decided to take a risk. It approached the entrance, which lay hidden behind the twisted girders and concrete that jutted out of the ruins like abstract sculpture. Instantly, the spotlight from the drone swung around and illuminated the hybrid. The spotlight remained fixed while the drone zipped over and hovered above the hybrid. A robotic voice spoke:

"Connection established. Identification successful. Welcome back, hybrid. Please enter."

Though relieved to have gained admittance to the pleasure den, the hybrid was shocked and disturbed to have been recognized by the drone's scanners. The hybrid was a fugitive and had long ago removed its GPS and identification implants. It had gotten used to traveling incognito, unrecognized by the tracking devices of the establishment. It was clear that the underworld had access to more sophisticated technology. The hybrid did not have time to be concerned about this, however. It needed to get its fix.

The hybrid walked through the entrance, camouflaged among the mangled piles of concrete and steel. A concealed panel slid open, revealing an elevator. The hybrid stepped in and the panel slid shut behind it. The elevator dropped rapidly and came to an abrupt stop. The panel slid open again and the hybrid stepped out.

The hybrid was greeted by a total sensory assault. It was now in the main chamber of the vast den, which was full of flashing lights and cacophonous sounds, not unlike the hotels in pre-war Las Vegas. The patrons – human, hybrid, and android – were involved in a variety of seedy activities. Many were sitting at gambling terminals and using biometric interfaces to play. Substances of all sorts were being consumed, from old-fashioned alcohol, amphetamines, and opiates to the newest designer chemical compounds. Some patrons drank, some smoked. Others snorted or injected. A few even connected directly to the dispensers via bio-ports, which was how the hybrid preferred to use.

In the many side rooms off of the main chamber, patrons engaged in sex acts of the strangest and most perverse kinds. Anything that could possibly be imagined could be experienced for a price. There were also rumors of seldom seen lower chambers, in which sadists and murders participated in truly dark and disturbing activities. The hybrid had no interest in any of that – it was solely focused on finding Tonik, and it had an idea about how to acquire some.

The hybrid crossed the floor of the main chamber quickly, heading straight to the back of the room. It came to a large door flanked by two burly and well-armed androids. As the hybrid approached, the androids moved in unison, stepping in front of the hybrid and blocking him from proceeding.

"What's your business?" demanded the android on the right.

"I'm here to see the boss," the hybrid replied. "I'd like to offer my services in exchange for payment."

"Have you worked for the Syndicate before?" asked the android on the left.

"Yes, many times. The boss has always been very pleased with my work."

"Yeah, I think I recognize you," the first android replied. "I'll see if the boss is available."

The android turned and knocked on the door. "There's someone here to see you, Boss. A hybrid. Says he worked with you before."

A voice called from beyond the door: "Excellent! Send him in."

The two androids stepped aside and the one on the right opened the door. The hybrid stepped through.

The boss' office was classically furnished and ornately decorated in rich shades of brown and burgundy. Fine art masterpieces hung on the walls. Statues carved by the hands of the Italian Renaissance masters stood in the corners of the room. The scent of old scotch and fine cigars hung in the air. Behind a large, oak desk sat the boss, a small man with a slick haircut and a very expensive suit.

"Please, come in," the boss said warmly. The hybrid entered the room. The androids shut the door behind him. "Ah, yes. I remember you," said the boss. "You did some jobs with the downtown crew. Ex-paramilitary, correct? Didn't you have a partner?"

"Yes, sir. He was killed earlier this evening on a bad gig. Some working-class meatbag was hiding a weapon. Got the jump on us."

"That's unfortunate. I hope you made him pay."

"Yes, sir," the hybrid lied.

"So, what can I do for you tonight? Are you looking for work?"

"I am, sir, but I have... a problem." The ache in the hybrid's head was increasing in intensity. A disconcerting, tingling electrical shock sensation now crackled in its brain stem, indicating rapid fluctuations in the signal between its brain and body.

"Oh, and what might that be?"

"I know you are a man who appreciates honesty, sir, so I'm just going to say it. I need a hit of Tonik and I need it now. Should have scored on that last gig but it went bad, so I have no money. I can offer you my services as payment."

"I see. I do indeed appreciate your candor, and I respect loyalty. You and your partner were good workers. It just so happens that an opportunity has opened up. I think you would be perfect for the job."

"That's great, sir. Anything."

"Why don't we get you fixed up first, and then we'll discuss business."

"Thank you, sir."

The boss reached over and opened a desk drawer on his right. He reached in and pulled out a long and intimidating device. It looked like a cross between a handgun and a hypodermic needle. He slid open a chamber on the top of the device and inserted a small, cylindrical cartridge. The cartridge snapped into place and the chamber automatically slid shut.

"You're going to like this," said the boss as he passed the grotesque device to the hybrid. "Our chemists have been tweaking the formula. This is the most potent batch we've ever created. Enjoy."

The hybrid had to refrain itself from greedily

snatching the device out of the boss' hands. Instead, it
politely received it and slowly, calmly pressed the protruding
needle into the carotid artery in what remained of its neck
and pulled the trigger. With a wet thump, the drug entered the
hybrid's system, shooting directly into its brain. Instant relief,
followed closely by an exploding, rushing euphoria made the
hybrid feel as if it were birthing galaxies in its head. It felt a
surge of power as a full connection between its body and
brain was re-established. Through the hazy fog of intense
pleasure, the hybrid could see the boss sitting behind the desk
with an amused expression on his face. The hybrid allowed
itself another brief moment to bask in the glorious sensations
before speaking. "Thank you, sir," it said. "That is some
really fine product. Now, how can I be of service?"

"I'm glad you enjoyed it," the boss smiled. "The task
is quite simple, really. I need you to escort an individual – an
asset of ours – to the Zone. He's been wiped and will be
heavily sedated. He should not put up a struggle. He will be
expected. Our observers will notify me upon his arrival.
Return when you are done and you will be payed
handsomely."

"Human?"

"Yes, but we expect great things of him. He's a natural
fighter and should produce excellent results. He's ex-
Resistance, and our scouting team feels like he could be the
best player to come along in many years. We are excited to
get him on the field."

"I'd be happy and honored to help, sir."

"Good. Check in with the boys outside and they'll get
you set up."

"Thank you, sir."

The hybrid stepped out of the office feeling
rejuvenated and exhilarated. The drug had worked its magic.
The dose would be effective for many hours, which would be

more than enough time to complete the task. The inevitable pain and discomfort it would feel when the chemical wore off was of no immediate concern.

"The boss wants me to escort someone to the Zone," the hybrid said to the androids outside of the office. "Ex-Resistance, apparently."

"Yeah, he's being held on the lower level," said the android on the left. "I'll take you to him."

"Have you ever been to the Zone?" the other android asked.

"I have, but it's been a long time," replied the hybrid.

"The game has changed. It's probably a lot more intense than you remember it. Spectators who get too close are likely to get killed. Be careful."

"I bet that's good for business. Viewership increasing?"

"Yeah, but the volatility makes it harder to control. The bookies are having a hard time. The house always wins, of course, but the profits have been slipping. This new player they're sending in – I'm sure it's a way of getting a grip on the fix again."

"I'm sure it is. I just want to get paid."

The hybrid and the android took a private elevator to the lower level. They disembarked and walked down a dark hall illuminated by red fluorescent tubes which ran along the ceiling. The unnerving sounds of unspeakable acts drifted through closed doors. A vile potpourri of scents hung in the stale air. They were traversing the underworld of the underworld. It was like an excursion through the infernal heart of Hell – a lucid nightmare.

The android and the hybrid reached a room near the end of the hall. The android waved a hand over a panel mounted on the wall and the door opened. They entered. The room was essentially a large kennel, but instead of cats or dogs, there were people – human and hybrid alike – inside the stacked cages. Most of them were clearly heavily sedated and unconscious. Some unfortunate individuals wavered on the threshold, their eyes dull and watery, low moans escaping their slack mouths. Only a few were fully awake and they sat hunched in their cramped cages, watching the hybrid and the android with blank expressions.

The android pointed to a cage and said, "That's the one. He's got a lot of spirit. We had to triple-dose him to get him to settle down. He's out now, but you better get him to the Zone quick. We'll provide you with transportation part of the way, but you'll have to go on foot for the rest."

The hybrid looked at the caged man and felt a momentary twinge of pity. It quickly disappeared. The hybrid had a job to do.

"I can handle him," the hybrid said. "I put down hundreds of 'em when I was on the Force. Let's just see how long he lasts in the Zone."

6

South of the city, accessible only by an old highway now closed to the public, was the entrance to the Zone. Only authorized vehicles and personnel were allowed to pass the checkpoint, which was situated at a bridge that crossed a deep and wide ditch. The ditch, and the barb wire fence on the other side, encircled the entire 10-square mile district. Only players entered. Only winners exited.

When Elden regained his senses, he found himself lying on a cot in what appeared to be a concrete bunker. Above him, a single light bulb hung from the ceiling. He was sore and disoriented. As he struggled to piece together what had happened before he had lost consciousness, a loud thud from a distant explosion somewhere above him shook the room. It caused the light bulb to swing wildly and cast ghastly shadows on the bare, gray walls. Elden sat up quickly, instantly alert and buzzing with adrenaline. *The Zone*, he thought. *Those fuckers sent me to the Zone.* Despite his kidnappers' attempts to wipe his mind, Elden retained his memories... and his indignation.

Elden stood from the cot and surveyed the room. On the wall opposite the cot there was a sink and a toilet, both practically antiques, cracked and coated in a thick layer of dark brown filth. Fetid water had pooled on the floor around the odious fixtures. To Elden's right, light from the street above streamed in through a small window high up on the wall. Below the window, leaning against the wall, was a military-grade, standard-issue rifle, beside which sat a soldier's rucksack, complete with sleeping bag and canteen. The rucksack was bulging with supplies and rations. There was a door on the wall opposite the window, which presumably led upstairs.

"I'll play your little game, you bastards," Elden said aloud as he picked up the rifle and rucksack and slung them over his shoulder. "I was born for this."

Elden checked the magazine of his weapon. It was full. He reinserted it and chambered a round. He then went to the door and put his ear to it, listening intently for any signs of activity beyond. Hearing nothing, he slowly turned the knob, pulled the door slightly ajar, and peered through the crack. He could see stairs leading up to an open landing. Elden opened the door fully and brought his rifle up into firing position. He crept up the stairs as silently as he could, his weapon ready, his senses keen, his mind hyper-vigilant.

At the top of the stairs, Elden peered over the landing, being careful not to expose himself to a potential ambush. He found himself looking into the ruins of what was once a spacious and comfortable living room. It was now a bombed-out, blackened, demolished husk. Destroyed furniture and the remnants of household items and personal mementos lay scattered among the debris. One of the walls had been entirely knocked out.

Satisfied that there was no immediate threat, Elden left the relative safety of the stairwell and entered the room. He went directly to a shattered window and looked out. The total destruction of his surroundings confirmed his suspicion – he was indeed in the Zone. The entire neighborhood lay in ruins. Each and every building had been bombed, blasted, and fought over countless times. It was a combat area, a brutal battlefield contained within the Zone's borders like an Armageddon-themed amusement park.

Elden had heard stories of the Zone from some of his former comrades in the Resistance. A few of them had been 'players' and had actually survived. He knew of many who had not. The totality of the destruction and the stark, hostile environment was still a shock to behold.

As Elden gazed out upon the battlefield – or what was essentially an arena for the players unlucky enough to find themselves drafted into the game, he spotted something that made him gasp. Towering into the sky, visible from miles away, was a gigantic, lumbering, robotic spider. It was an ominous sight, a surreal vision from a madman's dream. The dreadful contraption was taller than the largest buildings in the area that it apparently patrolled. The robotic spider moved like a daddy longlegs through the ruins and rubble of the Zone, bright spotlights shining down to the ground from its black metal chassis. It was searching for something, or someone.

"New tech," Elden muttered. "Looks like the game just got harder. Let's see what they gave me to work with."

Elden opened his rucksack and inventoried its contents. He was surprised to find it well-stocked with ammo, ready-to-eat meals, binoculars, matches, various utensils and tools, and other survival items. "Wouldn't be so entertaining for the bastards if I didn't have a fighting chance," he said as he packed everything up again and prepared to leave his current position. "Time to play."

Slipping out, Elden flowed into the front yard of the bombed-out home. He stayed low and close to the walls of the buildings as he made his way up the block. The home in which he had awoken was at the southern end of the Zone. The goal, as he understood it from the accounts of other survivors, was to reach a checkpoint somewhere at the far north. Exactly where, and what the final destination was, constantly changed. It was the gamekeepers' way of keeping it interesting and thwarting collaboration between old and new players, which would be, in their warped view, cheating.

As Elden neared the corner of the block, a loud droning sound alerted him to something passing over his head high above. The object was massive and cast a shadow that practically consumed him. It was directly over him, forcing him to tilt his head back at an extreme angle to get a look. What he saw was an incredibly large aerial vehicle hovering over his position. It was essentially a huge platform, arrayed with lights, cameras, and other sensitive viewing and recording equipment. As far as Elden could tell, it was remotely controlled and was used to observe and transmit what was happening in the Zone to spectators watching from the safety of homes and gambling establishments in the relatively secure districts of the city.

Elden waved at the platform and said, "You want a show? I'll give you a show. I'm ready for whatever you got. Bring it on, you bastards."

The hovering platform rapidly ascended and then suddenly blinked out of sight using its sophisticated cloaking capabilities. Elden knew that the craft would be watching everything he did – an invisible, dispassionate, omnipresent eye in the sky.

No sooner had the craft disappeared out of view when Elden's attention was immediately drawn to movement in the street. Something was approaching, rushing toward him in a furious, spinning blur. Elden quickly ran for cover beside the nearest home to his right. He crouched by the north wall, concealing his body, and watched as the strange, spinning object abruptly stopped in the intersection. It was only yards away, and Elden could now see that it was an autonomous robotic device shaped like a large wheel. On each side of the rotating main body were machine guns. The wheel rolled forward slightly and turned toward Elden's position. The guns remained fixed as the device moved, and now they were pointed directly at him.

Though the north wall of the home provided cover, the sight of the intimidating weaponry caused Elden to doubt the safety of his current location. He sprung into action and ran to the rear of the home. The robotic wheel opened fire just as he dashed away, obliterating the corner of the home in a deafening blast of rapid gunfire. The power of the weapons, and the damage they caused, momentarily stunned Elden. He paused behind the home and gathered his composure before sprinting around to the other side.

Elden could hear the robot whirring in the street. He moved up, staying flat against the wall. When he reached the wall's edge, he peered around the corner. He had a clear view of the machine. It was slowly rolling forward, toward the other side of the home. Elden went into action. He dropped to a crouching position, raised his rifle, and opened fire. The rounds from his weapon tore into the machine accurately and effectively. Elden kept firing until the robot's chassis began to smoke. It attempted to spin around to face him, but with another burst, Elden disabled it and the awful contraption toppled over on its side.

"Gotcha, you rusty piece of shit," Elden said as he reloaded his weapon.

The sun was rapidly setting. It would not be long before dusk fell upon the city. Elden watched the broken machine in the street for a few minutes. Once he was confident that the threat had been neutralized, he moved out of his position. His plan was to make as much progress as he could before dark. He had no idea how many miles away the final checkpoint was, but he had heard stories from those who had spent days and even weeks in the Zone. *I'm going to beat this game,* Elden resolved, *and I'm going to do it quickly and with style.*

For the next three hours, Elden moved through the Zone, working his way north. Over the course of his journey, he was stalked by a variety of robotic adversaries. In a multitude of forms, they pursued him relentlessly. Elden stayed hidden when he could, like a phantom among the ruined buildings, slinking and sneaking through the ragged shadows. It was impossible to avoid detection at all times, however, and he was forced to fight on a few occasions. He used his extensive combat training and advanced proficiency with his weapon to engage and destroy the threats that he could not evade.

By late evening, Elden had covered a fair distance and decided it was time to find shelter and get some rest. He chose a two-story building on a corner in what was once a middle-class neighborhood. The first floor had been a convenience store. The second floor contained living quarters for the family who had owned and operated the shop. Elden entered and went upstairs. Predictably, the small apartment was in total disarray. There were empty shell casings scattered among splintered furniture and shattered household items. The walls were pockmarked with bullet holes.

"Looks like there was a goddamn firefight in here," Elden muttered. "Must have been a real scrap."

Elden looked out a window and liked what he saw. He had a great view of the street. The position would be easy to defend, should he come under attack. He spread his sleeping bag out against the wall, sat down on it, and opened a ready-to-eat meal. He gobbled it down cold. He lay on his back, his rifle at his side and ready for action, and closed his eyes. He succumbed to his fatigue quickly, falling asleep within moments.

"Wake up, sleepyhead."

Elden returned to consciousness with a jolt. He reached for his rifle before his eyes were fully open, but it was gone. A man stood over him – he had Elden's rifle and was pointing it at Elden's forehead. "You fucked up, buddy," the man said. "I hate to do this, but I need your gear and weapon. Not everyone makes it out of here, you know. It's nothing personal. I just want to win."

The man pulled the trigger.

7

The simulation ended. Mickey lay in the holo-pod, momentarily confused. Emerging from a good program was always disorienting – the transition back to reality was a bumpy ride. Mickey's identity rushed back into his head like sea water into a tidal pool. *Wow*, he thought. *I didn't see that coming. I really thought I was gonna make it out of there. Poor Elden. Nice twist, though.*

Mickey remained in the holo-pod for a few more minutes, lying prone in the dark, savoring the incredible sensory experience he had just had. More compelling than a movie, more immersive than a video game, more thrilling than an amusement park ride – the simulations allowed the user to actually inhabit the characters and feel as if they were participating in the stories. The holo-pods were the state-of-the-art in entertainment technology. A good program made users totally forget their real lives and identities. A good program gave users the illusion of free will.

Mickey pressed a button on a panel to his left and the pod opened like a clam shell. He sat up, stretched his back, and rubbed his eyes. His stomach growled. He had been in the pod all evening and was now hungry and thirsty. Around him were other pods. The room was full of them. One by one they opened, revealing other users. Mickey turned to a woman seated in the pod next to him and said, "That was a wild one. How was it for you, Laura?"

"Intense," Laura replied as she climbed out of the pod. "Parts of it were really scary. Some of it made me sad."

"I liked the action," Mickey said. "Some really good fight scenes." He hopped out of his pod. He and Laura held hands as they walked to the exit of the pod room.

"It was more violent than I expected," Laura said. "I liked the little feral boy. I'm glad he found someone to take care of him."

Mickey and Laura merged with the crowd leaving the holo-pod theater. They stepped out onto the street. It was early morning.

"Wow, that was a long one," Laura noted. "I can't believe it's already morning."

"Let's catch a skybus and go home," said Mickey. "I need to eat and sleep."

Hand in hand, the couple walked two blocks up to the nearest boarding station. They got on the elevator and ascended to the upper platform. Once on top, they joined the others who were waiting beyond the gate. Just as everyone else did in such situations, they slid their E-visors into place. Among them stood a shy, anxious young man clutching a bagged lunch. He was not fully engrossed by the inner screen of an E-visor, because his had recently malfunctioned.

At precisely 8:15 AM, the skybus arrived at the boarding station. The nervous young man watched the skybus approach with naked, jittery eyes. He felt a strange sensation, like he had lived that moment before.

The Titan Taproom

On a rainy Wednesday evening in September, Luke and his friends gathered to enjoy a few beers at the Titan Taproom, a small, quaint neighborhood pub that served as their usual hangout. On this particular wet, cold, and gloomy night, only a handful of regulars had braved the weather to drink at the Titan. Luke, Bill and Jonathan, three close friends, were seated at a table close to the empty stage at the back of the pub. On the other side of the room, two other members of their close-knit group, Frank the Freak and Slow Tony, were playing a friendly, but competitive, game of eight-ball. The old man they all called Rummy Red was slouched at the bar, his stained and tangled beard dangling in his pint glass. Dean the Bartender was absentmindedly wiping the bar while watching a hockey game on a muted television set mounted above him. A Pink Floyd song played on the juke box, mingling and blending with the sound of the rain as it pounded the street outside.

So far that evening, the conversation at Luke, Bill, and Jonathan's table had been relatively normal – normal for them. In the middle of a discussion about a movie they had all recently seen, Luke suddenly made an astonishing announcement: "I have been contacted by an alien life form." Bill and Jonathan looked at him with blank expressions. It was not the first time Luke had said something bizarre. In fact, it was quite common, especially when they were having drinks at the Titan.

"Nice," said Bill.

"Sweet," said Jonathan.

"Yeah, it was pretty cool," Luke continued. "At first I

thought it was my imagination, but nope, it was *real*."

"Real like when you found the entrance to an underground laboratory in your backyard?" Bill snickered.

"Ha, ha, ha! I remember that," Jonathan said. "Wasn't it manned and operated by lizard people who promised not to hurt you if you didn't reveal the location?"

"Which, of course, he *did*," said Bill, shaking his head.

Luke ignored the gentle taunting. "The alien life form had some dire warnings for mankind," he said. "I've been asked to share its prophecies with my friends and family. Let me get another round and I'll tell you more."

Luke got up and went to the bar to order three more beers. Bill and Jonathan exchanged an amused glance. They watched in silence as Luke approached the bar, purchased the beverages, and returned to the table. Luke placed a bottle of beer in front of each of them, then sat down. "Drink up, brothers," he said. "I've got quite a story." Bill and Jonathan obliged, raising their bottles and taking a sip. Luke brought his own drink to his lips, tilted it nearly upside down, and poured half of it down his throat in one gulp.

"Okay, then," Luke said as he placed his elbows on the table, clasped his hands, and leaned in. "Are you ready for some hardcore truth?"

"Truth would be nice," Bill said. "I like truth."

"*You're* going to give us the truth?" Jonathan scoffed. "About what – the moon landing? The JFK assassination? What you had for dinner last night?"

"The truth about life and this reality," Luke said in an eerily calm voice. "Think you can handle it?"

"Just tell me this," Jonathan said with a hint of annoyance in his voice. "Where exactly did you encounter this 'alien' life form?"

"In the most unexpected and unusual place," Luke

said, "which is, apparently, where most alien life forms are found. This one was hiding under the sink in my apartment. Weird, eh?"

"Yes, Luke – that is pretty weird," Bill said as he took a big pull from his bottle of beer.

"Under your sink," said Jonathan. "You found an alien life form under your frickin' *sink*. Uh, huh... *right*."

"I didn't know what it was at first," Luke said. "I thought it was just a rotten old potato. It was squishy and moldy with nasty tendril-things growing out of it. I was going to just throw the damn thing in the garbage, but when I reached for it, it spoke."

"I gotta say, buddy, this is one of your more creative stories," Jonathan said.

"It's a good one," Bill agreed.

"There's more to it," Luke said. "It didn't just speak – it communicated directly with me – mind-to-mind, telepathically. Can you believe that?"

"Nope," said Bill and Jonathan in unison.

"The first thing it said was, 'Thank you.'" Luke paused for dramatic effect. He finished off his beer with another huge gulp before continuing. "The alien – I call it the Prophecy Potato – *thanked* me. Thanked *me*! I mean, *wow!*"

"I need a shot of whiskey," Jonathan muttered.

"I like that idea," said Bill.

Luke turned to face the bartender and shouted, "Dean, three whiskeys and three more beers! We're celebrating over here."

"What about us?" called Slow Tony from the pool table.

"I could use a drink," said Frank the Freak as he lined up his cue and sunk the striped eleven ball with a stylish, impressive bank.

"Sure, boys," Luke said. "It's a special occasion. A

round for everyone, Dean! Beers and whiskey. Make sure ol' Rummy Red gets in on this, too."

"Are you sure you can cover that, Luke?" Dean said. "You know I can't keep a tab for you anymore."

Luke dug around in the right front pocket of his jeans. He pulled out a crumpled wad of bills and flattened them on the table in front of him. "Fuckin' A!" he cried. "Almost 50 bucks! Now we're rockin' with Dokken. Pour us some bevvies, Dean!"

"Alright, but try to take it easy tonight, okay?" Dean lined up six shot glasses and filled them with whiskey. He retrieved six beers from the cooler and popped the caps, one by one. "I don't want another... incident," he said.

"Incident?" Bill asked curiously as he, Jonathan, and Luke rose from their seats and made their way to the bar. Frank the Freak and Slow Tony joined them. The five friends gathered around Rummy Red, who did not move, speak, or otherwise acknowledge their presence.

"It wasn't an *incident,*" Luke said. "That's a bit of an exaggeration, don't you think?"

Dean shook his head and smiled slightly. "I don't know, Luke. Jumping on a table and doing a rather raunchy striptease to some old '80s song *could* be considered an incident."

"Oh, come *on*, man!" Luke protested. "It was Saga's *On the Loose.* How could I resist? Who among us can honestly say they've never danced to that song? It's irresistible!"

"You're the only one I've seen go full frontal," Dean said. "And when you started spreading the ketchup on yourself..."

"I admit, that was a bit much. Anyway, cheers, boys!"

Luke paid for the beverages and then distributed the shots of whiskey. The five friends drank them down. Rummy

Red, who had remained seemingly motionless for the last few hours, finally moved. He guided the glass to his lips slowly with a shaky hand and took a sip.

"Whoa!" Luke exclaimed. "That hit the spot. Is that the good shit, Dean?"

"That's the cheapest we've got, Luke."

"Fair enough. Still damn tasty!"

Beers were then distributed. "Thanks for the drinks, Luke," said Bill. The others, with the exception of Rummy Red, who remained silent, followed suit and also expressed their gratitude. Slow Tony and Frank the Freak took their beers back to the pool table and resumed their game. Rummy Red finished his whiskey and started on his beer. Not once did he look at, or speak to, the young men who had congregated around him.

"Speaking of Saga, where are the tunes?" Luke said. "Who's got change?"

"I want to know more about the Prophecy Potato," said Bill.

"Yeah, so do I," said Jonathan. "It may be total bullshit, but at least it's *entertaining* bullshit this time."

"Patience, my friends," Luke said. "There's much more to the story, but I've got to set the scene. For that I need a good soundtrack." He wandered over to where the juke box rested against the wall. He provided a mumbled commentary as he scanned the selections: "That's a good one, but not quite right for this tale... Heard that one way too many times lately... Ride the Lightning – nice! Didn't know that one was in here. Not really appropriate, though... Lady fuckin' Gaga? Really? Who brought *that* shit in? Yuck... Ahh, this is the one – White Pepper. Perfect. You really can't go wrong with Ween, can you?" He slid a few dollars into the slot and within moments, the album began to play. The pounding, swirling, hypnotic rhythm of the opening track pulsed out of the speakers and filled the room. The atmosphere of the small pub was instantly transformed by the music.

Luke, Bill, and Jonathan took their beers back to their table and sat down. Outside, the rain still fell unabated, its persistent pitter-patter audible over the music. The crack of a cue hitting a pool ball reverberated as Slow Tony and Frank the Freak played on.

"Where was I?" asked Luke once the three young men had settled into their seats.

"In the middle of one of your fantasies," Jonathan quipped. "Something about an alien vegetable or some shit."

"The Prophecy Potato," Bill said, "it thanked you. You never told us why."

"I was getting to that," said Luke. He adjusted his position in his seat and rubbed his hands together. He took a deep breath and rolled his shoulders. "I've lived a strange life, as I'm sure you guys are well aware, but I never thought in my wildest dreams that something like *this* would happen to me. Who wants another shot of whiskey?"

"Just get to the point, Luke," Jonathan said.

"So, there I was last night, doing a little cleaning around the apartment."

"That's even harder to believe," sneered Bill. "Your place is filthy."

"I know," said Luke. "That's why I was cleaning. Anyway, there was a pungent stench coming from under the kitchen sink, so I opened the cabinet to take a look. That's when I found the potato."

"The Prophecy Potato," Jonathan said.

"Yes," Luke nodded. "That's what I call it. The name it gave me is totally unpronounceable in any human tongue."

"Care to try?" said Bill.

"If I did, I would probably rupture a vital organ or drop dead of an aneurysm," Luke replied.

"We wouldn't want *that* to happen," Jonathan said as he raised his beer bottle to his lips and took a substantial pull.

Luke resumed his narrative: "When I saw it, I sort of gasped. It was really a vile, repulsive sight. For a moment I wasn't sure if it was a dead rodent or a rotting piece of food. When I realized what it was, I was relieved. I was about to toss it in the trash when I heard something. That's the best way I can put it – I *heard* a voice, but it was non-localized. It seemed to be coming from nowhere and everywhere at once. The voice was in my head."

"I bet it was," Jonathan said with a roll of his eyes.

"It was clearly separate from my own thoughts," Luke continued. "I knew immediately that the thing under the sink was communicating with me. 'Thank you!' it said. 'I've been trapped here for weeks and thought I'd never be found. You saved me! Thank you!'"

"You're a frickin' hero," Jonathan grumbled.

Luke pressed on with his story: "After I got over the initial shock of the encounter, I decided not to tell the thing that I had planned to throw it away. Instead, I reached in, picked it up gently, and placed it on the counter. 'Ahh,' it moaned with pleasure in my head, 'it's so nice to get out of that cabinet. You should really fix the pipes in there. You've got a serious leak. And the bugs! Have you considered getting an exterminator? I had roaches crawling all over me. Disgusting.'"

"See, I *told* you your apartment was filthy," Bill said. "Even the rotten potato found the conditions you live in appalling."

"It's true. My place is a mess... but to be admonished by a sentient, telepathic vegetable was highly unusual."

"It's never happened to me," replied Bill, "and my place can get pretty messy at times. Not like the squalor you live in, but it's not exactly a sterile clinic either."

"After it reprimanded me," Luke said, "the potato made me an offer: 'If you hadn't released me from the terrible confines of that awful prison under the sink, I would have met my sure demise. For that, you have my sincere gratitude. I would also like to offer you something much more valuable. How would you like to have access to a source of knowledge so vast and immense that it would, in effect, make you omniscient. More than that – its application would make you *omnipotent*. How does that sound?"

"You're already impotent," snapped Jonathan.

"*Om*nipotent," Bill corrected him. "It means all-powerful."

"Yes, that's right," Luke said. "I was intrigued, of course. I was about to ask the potato what it wanted from me, but I didn't have to. The thing could read my thoughts. Before I said anything, I heard its voice in my head: 'All you have to do is keep me safe here in your apartment. Find a nice cardboard box and keep me somewhere cool and dry. If you could occasionally trim my sprouts, too, that would be much appreciated. In return, I will reveal to you things that have yet to pass. Through me, you will have a window into the future.'"

"Sounds pretty tempting!" cried Bill.

"That's what *I* thought," said Luke.

Jonathan shook his head and sighed. "I think I *will* need another drink. Next round is on me." He got up and went to the bar.

"He doesn't believe me," Luke said to Bill in Jonathan's absence.

"Doesn't matter," said Bill. "It's a good story."

Jonathan returned to the table with three more beers. He passed them around and the friends took synchronized sips.

"So, did you agree to the potato's terms?" Bill asked.

"I was thinking about it when the voice said, 'You've already made up your mind. That is a wise decision that you will not regret.' So, yes, I did agree to its terms."

"That thing is in your apartment right now?" Bill asked, giving Luke a quizzical look.

"Yes, and it is quite comfortable, too," Luke nodded. "I made a little bed for it out of a box and a T-shirt. I trimmed its sprouts just before I left to come here. It seemed to really like that. I thought I could hear it purring gently in my head."

"Oh, for fuck's sake..." Jonathan was getting irritated and surly. "What a load of shit. Usually I like your stories, Luke, but this one is just too much. I might be the only one who cares enough about you and has the guts to actually say this, but you are not well, buddy. You need professional help. Have you considered seeing a shrink? Maybe getting on some meds?"

"I don't know about *that*," Bill said in an attempt to keep the conversation positive, "but what you're telling us is pretty far-fetched, Luke. We're all a little concerned about your... imaginative stories lately. I enjoy hearing them, but sometimes we get a little scared for your well-being. It's because we care about you."

"Thanks, guys," Luke smiled, "but I'm doing just fine. Really, I am. If you want to know another secret, very soon we will have confirmation of the powers of the Prophecy Potato." Luke glanced up at a clock on the wall behind him. "In approximately five minutes, actually. Just watch the door and you will see for yourself."

Bill and Jonathan reflexively turned to face the pub's entrance. "What the hell are you talking about now?" Jonathan asked. "Did that thing make some kind of prediction?"

"Let's just say that the night is about to get a lot more interesting," Luke replied.

The three men at the table sat watching the entrance. Bill and Jonathan, despite their skepticism, experienced an uncanny sense of anxious anticipation. Jonathan tried to shrug it off. "This is so frickin' stupid," he mumbled. Bill simply stared with one eyebrow raised. Luke calmly took a sip from his bottle of beer. Abruptly, the door flew open and a gust of wind swept through the room, bringing with it a cold mist and the sound of the relentless, hammering rain. Startled, Bill and Jonathan jumped in their seats. "Two minutes earlier than I expected," Luke said. "It's not an exact science."

Through the open door stepped a tall figure. It was a man in a tasseled leather jacket and black jeans. He wore a dark leather cowboy hat pulled low over his eyes. The spurs on the heels of his steel-toed, snakeskin cowboy boots jangled loudly. The man tipped his hat back, looked around the room, and said, "What's up, pussies?"

"Shut the damn door, Richie," Dean the Bartender said. Richie grudgingly obliged.

"Oh, great," said Bill, just loud enough for those at his table to hear. "This guy is a real tool."

"*This* is your prophecy?" Jonathan smirked. "Richie makes a dick of himself at the Titan *every* night. Doesn't take a prophet to predict that."

"Let's just see what happens, shall we?" Luke replied.

Richie swaggered up to the bar, sat on a stool beside Rummy Red, and slapped his hat down on the counter. "Gimme a gin and tonic," he said. "Make it a double."

"You do realize I have the right to refuse you service, right?" Dean asked.

"Do *you* realize I have the right to refuse you oxygen?" Richie snapped.

"Is that supposed to be a threat? What does that even *mean?*"

"Ahh, I'm just teasin', Dean. All in good fun. We're buds, aren't we? It's cold and rainy out there. Hook up an old friend with a drink, will ya? I need to warm my guts."

"Ugh," Dean groaned. "Sometimes I wonder what the hell I'm doing with my life. There's got to be more to it than serving booze to ungrateful mouth-breathers every night."

In a smooth, quick series of well-practiced moves, Dean prepared a double gin and tonic. He placed the glass on a napkin in front of Richie. "Just don't make a *total* ass of yourself tonight, okay?" he pleaded.

"You seem tense," Richie said as he raised the glass and took a sip. "Relax. Have a drink. Unbunch your panties, bro. Life is too short to be uptight."

"It's going to be a long night," Dean sighed. He took Richie's advice and poured himself a shot of whiskey. He tossed it back and turned his attention to the televised hockey game. The Oilers were beating the Flames three to two.

"How are you doing tonight, Red?" Richie addressed Rummy Red, who was sitting on the stool directly to his right, slumped over the bar and nursing his beer. "Gettin' any action lately?" Richie teased. Rummy Red did not respond. "I could sure use some action," Richie said as he spun around on the stool. He spotted Luke, Bill, and Jonathan. Luke, Bill, and Jonathan were looking at him. Richie put his cowboy hat back on, got up, and approached their table.

"Crap," Bill murmured. "Here comes a walking, talking cliché."

"I'm not putting up with his shit tonight," said Jonathan. "If he says anything even *remotely* stupid, I'm going to knock him on his ass."

"Be careful," Luke said. "The Prophecy Potato warned me about this. Something bad is going to happen."

Richie walked up and stood looming over the three men at the table. "You dickholes gonna offer me a seat or what?"

"Wasn't planning on it," Bill said.

"I wasn't planning on planting my boot in your ass, but that just might happen anyway," spit Richie.

"What is your *problem?*" Jonathan spat back. "We were having a good time until your sorry ass walked through the door."

"A good time? With *Luke?*" Richie's face distorted in an exaggerated grimace. "How could you? That dude is batshit crazy."

Luke smiled and took a sip of his beer. He set the bottle down and said, "Have a seat, Richie. Join us."

"Alright, yeah," Richie said as he slid into a chair between Bill and Jonathan. "Luke might be nuts, but at least he has some common fucking decency. That's more than I could say about you two fart jars."

"So, what's new with you, Richie?" Bill asked tentatively. It was a dangerous question.

"Been kickin' ass and taking names, as usual." Richie replied.

"Still pumping gas for a living?" Jonathan asked.

"None of your business, goof."

"He is," Slow Tony answered from the pool table. "He gave me a fill-up the other day. Washed my windows and checked the oil, too."

"Did you tip him?" Jonathan called back.

"I gave him a couple of bucks. I figured he could use the change."

"You guys better watch your mouths," Richie said through clenched teeth. His face was now a dramatic shade of red. "You don't want to piss me off tonight."

"Hey, take it it easy, fellas," Luke said. "We're all friends here, aren't we? Who wants another drink?"

"This round's on me," said Richie, gaining his

composure. "I'm here to celebrate. I got some kickass news today. You ass noodles are in for a fucking *surprise.*" Richie reached into his pocket and produced a massive handful of change, presumably acquired from tips while working as a gas station attendant. "Dean, beers for the boys and another double gin and tonic for me!" he yelled.

"You gonna come here and get them?"

"I worked my ass off all day," Richie said. "Why don't *you* do some actual work for a change and bring us the friggin drinks?"

"I'm warning you..." Dean started to say.

"I'll get them," Luke said, rising from his seat. "No worries."

"Take this." Richie dumped the change into Luke's cupped hands. "Should be plenty there. Let Deaner have whatever is left. I'm feeling generous today."

Luke paid for the drinks and carefully transported them back to the table. With a fresh beverage in front of each of the seated imbibers, Richie launched into his story:

"I was working a 3-11 shift the other day, and while I was sittin' in the kiosk eating some jerky, a brand new Benz pulled up to the pumps. It was a car I hadn't seen before. I'd have remembered it – not too many people in this sorry-ass excuse for a town can afford wheels like that. It looked fresh off a showroom floor. The windows were tinted, so I couldn't see in. I walked up to the driver's side window and it rolled down. The dude inside was real sharp lookin' – dark shades, slicked-back hair, silk shirt, sports jacket. I said, 'Fill 'er up?' He just kinda smiled in this really confident but sorta spooky way. I said, 'Need some gas, mister?' Then he pulled his sunglasses down until his eyes were peeking over the top of them and said, 'This vehicle does indeed need gas, but I, my friend, need something much more rare and valuable – I need young men like you. Are you interested in the opportunity of a lifetime?'"

"Sounds like a diddler to me," said Jonathan.

"That's what I thought." Richie nodded solemnly. "So I just ignored the comment and asked him how much gas he needed. He told me to fill it up, so I did. When I went to his window to get paid, he still had that weird smile on his face. He handed me a credit card and said, 'There's something special about you. I can always tell.'"

"Special needs, maybe," Bill chuckled.

"Laugh it up, assholes," Richie said. "You won't be laughing for much longer. The dude in the Benz asked me if I had ever wanted to be anything more than a pump jockey. 'Well, yeah,' I told him. 'I've got big plans for my future.' 'Like what?' he asked, so I said, 'I'm a guitar player. I'm going to be rich and famous some day.' The dude grinned real big. He had perfect, white teeth – almost too perfect. I bet he paid big bucks for them. He seemed to like my answer to his question. 'Good for you,' he said. 'Speak it into existence.'"

"This is almost as crazy as Luke's potato story," Jonathan said with a shake of his head. "You think you're going to be a rock star or something? You can't even *play*. I gotta be honest – you truly suck."

"You don't know shit," said Richie. "Sometimes I wonder why I even hang out with you guys."

"Because no one else can tolerate you," replied Bill.

"I can barely tolerate him, that's for sure," Jonathan muttered.

"It's fate," Luke said. "We have no choice. Destiny brought us together for a reason."

Richie, Jonathan, and Bill stared at Luke for a moment before cracking up in an eruption of laughter. The cackling continued for many minutes before petering out. Even Luke found himself giggling by the time the uproar had ended.

"Fate... destiny. That's hilarious," wheezed Jonathan. "So, tell me, Richie, what did this spooky rich dude tell you?"

"He told me that he that he had the power and connections to make my wildest dreams come true. He told me that he could make me a rock star."

"And you believed him?"

"Not at first, but the more we talked, the more I was convinced. It's hard to explain, but he has a real... *presence*. You fools will see for yourselves soon enough – he's meeting me here tonight. He should be walking through that door any time now."

It was an innocuous statement, but Richie's words resonated with an ominous tone. A hush fell upon the men at the table. For a few strange, silent moments, they nervously sipped their drinks and cast tense glances around the room. The crack of pool balls colliding resounded from the back of the tavern as Slow Tony took a shot. He missed, cursed, and then wandered over to the juke box still holding his cue. He inserted some money into the machine and soon *Jockey Full of Bourbon* by Tom Waits filled the room, adding to the surreal ambiance.

> *Edna Million in a drop-dead suit*
> *Dutch Pink on a downtown train*
> *Two-dollar pistol but the gun won't shoot*
> *I'm in the corner in the pouring rain*
> *Sixteen men on a dead man's chest*
> *And I've been drinking from a broken cup*
> *Two pairs of pants and a mohair vest*
> *I'm full of bourbon, I can't stand up*

"Sometimes I swear I'm living in The Twilight Zone," Bill said.

"You are," said Luke. "The world is weirder than you ever imagined – weirder than you *can* image."

"You're creepin' me out, man," Bill replied.

"I just came here to drink," Jonathan said as he guzzled his beer. "You weirdos are letting your imaginations get the best of you. I expect that from Luke, but you two –" Jonathan gestured at Bill and Richie, "– are acting like sissies. Delusional sissies."

It was then that the door once again swung open with a blast of cold, wet air and the sound of the unceasing rain. Again, all eyes – with the exception of the two dull, milky orbs that sat in the eye sockets of Rummy Red – turned to the entrance. A man stepped into the tavern. "There he is," said Richie. "I knew he would show up."

The man fit the description of the man whom Richie had met at the gas station – he was of average height and average build, but he had the chiseled features and confident expression of a man who knew what he wanted and was used to getting exactly that. He wore an overcoat and carried an umbrella, which retracted with the push of a button on the handle as he entered. The door shut behind him and the man ran a hand through his slicked-back hair while he scanned the room with bright blue, penetrating eyes. The 'presence' that Richie had described was palpable.

The man at the door spotted the four men at the table near the center of the room. "Richie!" he exclaimed. "How are you this fine evening? May I join you and your friends for a beverage?"

"Yeah, man," Richie replied. "That's cool with me. Is it cool with you guys?"

Luke, Bill, and Jonathan nodded their approval.

"Excellent!" cried the man in the wet overcoat. "Bartender, a glass of your finest red wine, please."

"You got it, mister," said Dean. The wine was served

and the man brought his glass to the table. He gracefully slid into an empty seat between Luke and Jonathan. "Greetings and salutations, my young friends," he said. "My name is Stan."

"Right on, brother," said Richie. "Thanks for coming. Did you have trouble finding the place?"

"No, Richie, I did not," replied Stan. "Although I do not *frequent* this area of town, I will admit that I am not entirely unfamiliar with it either. I have met many of my clients in establishments such as this."

Stan removed his overcoat, revealing an expensive, deep-red silk shirt. It was the color of fresh blood pumped directly from the heart. Stan carefully draped the overcoat on the back of his chair. He took a sip of wine – it, too, was the color of arterial blood. Stan spoke: "Richie, are you going to introduce me to your friends?"

"These bozos? Sure. Jonathan is the mopey one with the goatee and the Morbid Angel shirt. Bill is the little guy in the white hoodie. The crazy-looking dude with the wild eyes is Luke."

Jonathan, Bill, and Luke smiled and nodded their understated greetings. Stan studied each of their faces closely, his eyes intense and piercing. It was as if he was trying to infiltrate their minds and peer into their very souls. After scrutinizing the men at the table, Stan's face loosened and his body relaxed. "It's very nice to meet all of you," he said. "Has Richie informed you of how we met and the nature of this rendezvous?"

"He mentioned something about filling your tank and discussing a possible career change," Bill said.

"I *bet* he filled his tank," chuckled Jonathan. "Filled it all night long."

"Yes, we did indeed meet at his current place of employment," said Stan, gracefully disregarding Jonathan's

innuendo. "I immediately recognized his inherent potential.
Richie is a special young man with the ability to transcend
his current station in life. He simply needs an opportunity to
cultivate and express his latent genius."

"*Genius?*" cried Jonathan. "Are you friggin' kidding
me? Richie is about as smart as a bag of hammers. *Genius* –
give me a break."

"Richie possesses an uncommon and beautiful gift,"
Stan said. "It is unfortunate that his environment has not been
more supportive."

"I always knew I was gonna make something of
myself," Richie mused.

"Can this night get any more *insane?*" said Bill.

Luke, who had been silently observing Stan since he
arrived, finally spoke up: "It can, and it will, won't it, Stan?
Why don't you tell us exactly what it is that you plan to do
for Richie? He seems to think you're going to transform him
into some kind of rock n' roll demigod."

"*Rock n' roll demigod*," Stan grinned. "I like that. The
reality is a little more mundane. I simply have the
connections and resources to nurture Richie's talents and take
his career to the next level... if he so wishes, of course. The
decision is his to make."

"Yeah, man. I can dig it," said Richie.

"Have you ever even heard him *play?*" asked
Jonathan. "I have. He's terrible. I mean *really* shitty.
Remember the last open mic you did, Richie? Here on that
very stage? No one could tell if you were playing a song or
tuning your guitar or torturing a small animal to death. It was
horrendous. He got booed off the stage. Remember that,
Richie?"

"It was a new song, a work in progress, asshat,"
mumbled Richie.

"His current level of skill on his chosen instrument is

irrelevant," replied Stan. "There are more important factors to consider."

"Like what?" Bill asked.

"Commercial viability, for instance," Stan replied. "Which itself is a complicated and mysterious collection of factors. It is very hard to quantify, but I knew immediately, the first time I laid eyes on him, that Richie has commercial viability. It's in the way he looks, talks, dresses, and carries himself. More than that – it is a deeply inherent trait that only a select few in my industry are able to detect. Richie was *born* to be a star."

"Fuckin' A, man," said Richie.

"What a load of horseshit," Jonathan sneered.

"Would you like a demonstration of what I am able to do for my clients?" Stan asked. "I think you'll be amazed at the... transformation."

A quiet, mostly ambivalent murmur of consent from the men at the table prompted Stan into action. In a swirling, dramatic display of motion, he swallowed the last of his red wine, rose from his seat, and circled the table like a dust devil spinning across a desert highway. He stopped and stood behind Richie completely still with his hands raised, his eyes closed, and his head tilted back. A strange sound rose from Stan's throat, audible not through his mouth, but directly from his throbbing Adam's apple. The sound was eerie and disturbing, like an approaching cloud of locusts. A distant, detached expression slackened Richie's face. Luke, Bill, and Jonathan could only stare in stunned silence at the unusual scene unfolding before them. Stan waved his hands in a final flourish, then opened his eyes. The short and spooky ritual was over. Richie shuddered and seemed to regain awareness. Stan returned to his seat.

"What was *that* supposed to be?" Jonathan asked.

"I feel... different," said Richie. "I feel *good.*"

"As you should, my young star in the making," Stan smiled. "You told me earlier that you would be willing to audition for me. I've been led to believe there is an instrument and a stage available upon these premises. Is that correct?"

"Yeah, dude. There's a house guitar up there for the open mic people." Richie pointed at the darkened stage. "It's kinda shitty and a little beat-up, but it works."

"As if that matters," said Jonathan. "It all sounds like noise when you play the thing."

"I'd like to hear for myself," Stan said. "Richie, would you be so kind as to get up there and play a song for us?"

"Sure... if that's cool with Dean." Richie looked to the bartender for approval. Dean, without taking his eyes off the hockey game on the television, waved a hand absentmindedly.

"I guess that means it's okay," Richie shrugged.

"Marvelous," smiled Stan.

"Oh, God," said Jonathan. "This should be entertaining."

"I have no doubt about that," Luke said. "I think we are in for quite a show indeed."

Richie rose from his seat and walked toward the stage. "Hey, Dean, how about some power?" he called as he climbed up. Dean flicked a switch and the stage was bathed in colored light. At stage right was an old, red Stratocaster sitting in a stand beside a battered amplifier. Richie picked up the guitar and slung the strap over his shoulder. He plugged a cable leading to the amplifier into the body of the guitar and turned the amp on. The sound of static rumbled from the speaker. Richie tentatively strummed a chord. It was loud and crunchy. With a few twists of the machine heads, Richie tuned the instrument to his satisfaction. He walked to the edge of the stage and looked out upon his small audience.

"This is a dirty little jam I've been working on," he announced.

Striking an exaggerated Guitar Hero pose, Richie began to play. A chaotic, cacophonous, jumbled series of sloppy riffs and discordant notes burst forth from the amplifier. The sound was dissonant, unnerving, and painful. Richie began banging his head and flailing about, immune to the tuneless racket he was creating.

"Just as shitty as ever," Jonathan observed.

"Somehow he got worse," Bill said. "How is that even *possible?*"

As Richie continued to play, an amazing thing happened. The notes began to coalesce into something approximating music. The rough and raunchy chords and seemingly arbitrary rhythms formed themselves into logical and ear-pleasing arrangements. Out of the awful din, a structured and melodic sound was emerging, like an extra-dimensional interloper. Just as Stan had predicted, an obvious transformation was occurring. The noise morphed into music. Richie now had the attention of everyone in the room.

"Well, shit," said Jonathan with a look of total bewilderment on his face. "I guess he's been practicing."

"I heard him play just last week," Bill said. "It was crap."

"It's almost miraculous," said Luke.

On the stage, Richie was really rocking now. His fingers flew up and down the neck, performing complicated and elaborate moves with precision and ease. The music grew more intense. Baroque flourishes of notes and wild ascending and descending phrases pulsed from the speaker of the amplifier. The small audience was captivated. Richie, too, seemed surprised and confused by what was happening. He was watching his hands intently as if they no longer belonged to him – as if they were possessed. With a final, screaming bent note, Richie's performance ended. The last note hung in the air, echoing through the room and in the minds of the astonished audience.

It took a few moments for Richie to recover. With his head down and breathing heavily, he stood on the stage cradling the guitar. Finally, he gathered his composure, slid out of the strap, and gently placed the instrument back on its stand. Richie stepped off the stage in an apparent daze and returned to the table.

As Richie sat back down, Stan slapped him warmly on the back and said, "Well done, my young star! That was brilliant. I knew you had it in you. Are you ready to see the world and perform for thousands of adoring fans?"

"Well, uh, yeah," Richie stammered. "Somethin' kinda weird happened while I was up there. It's like the music took control of my body."

"That's what it *should* do," smiled Stan. "Music is a profoundly powerful medium. When used correctly, it can be a real force for change – emotional, psychological, spiritual, even political. The influence that music can have on people should not be underestimated."

"What in the fuck did I just witness?" cried Jonathan. "Richie walks in here like some thrift store, talentless, heavy metal wannabe and suddenly transforms into Eddie Van-friggin-Halen? Is anyone else a little freaked out by this?"

"We were warned," Luke stated gravely. "The Prophecy Potato *told* me something like this would happen tonight."

Bill rubbed his eyes with the palms of his hands and said, "Did someone put LSD in my beer?"

Stan turned to the bar, raised an arm, and addressed Dean, who, despite the highly unusual display that had just transpired on his stage, was still transfixed by the televised hockey game. "Bartender, another round of whatever these gentlemen have been drinking, and another glass of that delectable red wine for me, if you please!"

Dean began to slowly gather bottles and glasses and arranged them on the bar. He managed to keep his eyes locked on the television while he worked. The Oilers had tied the game and it was about to go into overtime.

"Pour and serve with haste and there's a $100 tip in it for you!" called Stan. Dean instantly switched his full attention to the task at hand. With blazing speed, he popped caps, poured wine and liquor, and placed the bottles and glasses on a tray. He trotted over to the table and set the tray down. "That's more like it," Stan said. "A jump in your step and some fire in your eyes – it's amazing what a crisp, brown bill can do for a man, isn't it?" Stan pulled a one hundred dollar bill out of his wallet and handed it to Dean, who received it eagerly. Stan winked as he completed the transaction and said, "Do make sure the elderly man at the bar isn't left thirsty, will you, please? He looks like he could use another drink."

"You got it," replied Dean as he folded the bill and tucked it into his pocket. "If you need anything else, let me know." Dean went back to his position behind the bar and gave Rummy Red another bottle. The men at the table picked up their drinks.

"I propose a toast," Stan said, raising his glass of wine. "Here's to new friendships, new careers, and the beginning of a wonderful and potentially lucrative partnership!"

"Cheers, buddy," said Richie, sipping his gin. Jonathan and Bill guzzled their beers. Luke pressed a finger against his lips and stared firmly at Stan.

"That was quite a show, Richie," Luke said, his eyes still locked on Stan. "I don't think I've ever seen anyone improve so much so quickly. Truly extraordinary."

"Yeah, man," said Richie. "I guess all those hours of practice are finally paying off."

"Yes, maybe," Luke said, "or perhaps there's more to your new friend and benefactor than meets the eye. Isn't that right, Stan?"

Stan chuckled and said, "Well, we *all* have our secrets, but I assure you, I mean you and your friends no harm. I merely seek new talent. I wish only to nurture and refine Richie's gifts before presenting him on the world stage. As you have clearly seen, he has abundant star power. Now he needs proper management."

"What's in it for you?" asked Luke.

"Money, of course, but also other intangibles," Stan replied. "If the project is successful – and it will be – my associates and I will have the distinct and delicious pleasure of contributing something of real *substance* to this culture. It is tremendously satisfying."

"*Substance?*" Jonathan cried. "Richie has about as much substance as a fuckin' fart."

Stan laughed heartily. "That's quite humorous. Thank you. The truth is, however, that one must be prepared – groomed – for the world stage. That is where my associates and I come in. We have years – decades, really – of experience. We have been transforming regular mortals into god-like celebrities for a very long time."

"That sounds pretty sweet," said Richie. "Think I'll get laid a lot? What about blow? I bet I'll be rollin' in it."

"Oh, yes," Stan said. "Women, drugs, money – all of these things and more will be yours in abundance once we get the contract worked out."

"Fuckin' A!" shouted Richie.

"What else does Richie have to do, other than look good in leather and play his guitar?" Luke asked. "Who writes the songs?"

"We have a team of professionals who take care of that," Stan said. "They are the elite of the industry. They are the architects of the cultural zeitgeist. Songwriting is not something Richie will ever have to be concerned with. In fact, he will be required to perform only the material we provide him with. It's part of his contractual obligations."

"Doesn't seem very creatively satisfying to me," said Luke.

"This business is not about creativity," Stan replied. "It is about making money... and reaching the hearts and minds of young people."

"That's cool with me," shrugged Richie. "I just wanna get out there and rock."

"And so you shall," Stan smiled. "We already have some material prepared for you. I think you will quite like it."

"I hope it's not crappy pop shit," said Richie.

"Far from it," Stan said. "In fact, I think you will be quite pleased with the direction we are taking with this project. Sex, death, drugs, nihilism – good, fun, old-fashioned rock n' roll. We're going to return to the basics."

"Right on, man!" Richie was delighted. "I love that kind of shit."

"Yes, I thought you might," Stan said. "The next step in the process is to get you signed. It just so happens that I have a contract here with me. How would you like to make this arrangement formal, right here, right now?"

"Sure! What have I got to lose?"

"How about your soul. Do you value that?" A voice called out from somewhere near the bar. The men at the table turned, and each and every one of them was surprised to see that the individual who had just spoken was Rummy Red, who, until that moment, had remained utterly silent and nearly motionless.

"It's time for this awful charade to end," said Rummy Red, rising from the bar stool to which he had been plastered the entire night. "I know who you are, Stan, and I'm not going to let you get away with what you are trying to do."

Everyone in the bar was now staring at Rummy Red, baffled, stupefied, astounded – everyone, that is, except Stan, who crossed his arms across his chest, cocked his head to one side, and said, "What, exactly, is it that you think you know, old man? Mind your own business."

"This man is not to be trusted," Rummy Red said to the group as he approached the table.

"Coming from you, that's pretty funny," chuckled Richie. "Seriously, though, we're having an important discussion here. Go back to your stool."

"I've been coming here for a long time," Bill said to no one in particular, "and I've never heard Rummy Red speak. I didn't think he *could* speak. I just assumed his brain was basically soggy oatmeal."

"The plot sickens," said Jonathan.

"Red, what are you trying to say?" Luke asked.

"This man is evil incarnate," replied Red. "Can't you see? I wouldn't believe a single word that comes from his rotten, lying, serpentine mouth."

"I think I've heard enough from this paranoid old wino," Stan said with a dismissive wave of his hand. "Let's continue with the business at hand, shall we?"

Stan reached into the inner pocket of the overcoat draped over his chair and retrieved a large manila envelope that had been tucked inside. He unwound the string holding the clasp shut and pulled out a multi-page, stapled document. As Stan was about to lay the document on the table in front of Richie, Red suddenly snatched the pages out of his hands with the speed and precision of a kung fu master. Before Stan could react, Red viciously tore the pages into pieces and threw them on the floor in disgust.

Stan stood up and faced Red, his expression now radiating rage and contempt. "You just made a huge mistake, old man."

Red stood his ground defiantly. "What are you going to do about it? You think I'm afraid of you? You were a cowardly piece of demonic trash in '66 and you still are. I kicked your ass then and I can do it again."

Stan howled with malevolent laughter. "We meet again, my dear friend and nemesis. My sincere apologies for not recognizing you sooner. The years haven't been kind to you."

"Not surprisingly, you look exactly the same," Red said. "Still drinking the old youth juice, I see."

"Of course! There's an endless supply of it on this fallen, wretched planet. More than ever, actually. People are practically *begging* to give it away these days."

Stan and Red stood facing each other. Every other person in the bar was frozen, rapt and riveted by the unfolding confrontation. The atmosphere in the room was thick and heavy. Outside, the rain still pounded the street relentlessly. The moment stretched out, long, tense, pregnant with an imminent explosion.

"So, what happens now?" Stan finally asked.

"I think you know the answer to that," Red replied.

"Yes, I believe I do."

In a wild flash, Red launched his attack, opening with a rapid, powerful jab to Stan's right cheekbone. Flesh split and bones crunched. Stan tottered on his feet momentarily before counterattacking with an equally vicious uppercut that knocked Red on his ass. With strength and speed that defied his appearance, Red jumped to his feet swinging. Luke, Bill, Jonathan, and Richie managed to vacate their seats just as Red landed a series of blows that sent Stan crashing onto the table. The table collapsed. Glass shattered and wood splintered. The men who had been seated moved away from the melee.

"Hey! Hey!" shouted Dean from behind the bar. "Stop that shit! Take it outside!"

The fighters paid no heed. Stan was back on his feet and ready for more. Red stood waiting in a defensive stance. Stan flew at Red with a roar. With a deft twist of his body, he surprised Red with a brutal sidekick to the upper chest. Red was thrown halfway across the room, landing hard and awkwardly on the pool table between Frank the Freak and Slow Tony.

"Ouch," said Frank.

"You okay, buddy?" asked Tony.

Red lay on the table panting for a few moments before pulling himself up and jumping down. "I'd stay out of the way if I were you," he said. Red brushed himself off and walked toward Stan, who was waiting patiently near the debris of the destroyed table with an amused expression on his face.

"You never know when to give up," Stan said, shaking his head.

"Let's finish this," replied Red.

"With pleasure."

Stan swiftly reached down and picked up a large section of the split table top and swung the jagged piece with all his might at Red's head. With a sickening crack, the heavy wood connected with skull and Red was once again on the floor. A collective gasp rose from the shocked spectators. Red lay immobile where he had fallen, blood streaming from a large gash across his left temple.

"What the fuck, dude!" shrieked Richie. "You killed him!"

"The cops are on their way," Dean called from behind

the bar.

"Just another night at the Titan," remarked Jonathan.

"He's not dead," Stan said. "Are you, old friend?"

Red stirred, slowly sat up, and gently probed the open wound on the side of his head. "Got a bit of a headache, but I'm still among the living," he said.

"Among the living – that's a good way of putting it," Stan said. "I don't know about you, but I'm starting to find this very boring. It's monotonous, really. What are we doing here? *Why?*"

With a drawn-out grunt, Red got to his feet. He brushed the dust from his shoulders and chest and ran a hand through his bloodied beard. He looked Stan directly in the eyes and addressed him with sincerity: "I've got to be honest – I have no idea what you see in this one." A toss of his head indicated he was referring to Richie. "I think you might be losing your touch."

"I admit," Stan said, "I'm scraping the bottom of the barrel with this specimen, but a soul's a soul."

"Huh? What?" muttered Richie. "Are they talking about me?"

"I think so, big guy," said Jonathan with a slap on Richie's back.

"Praise the potato," Luke said. "I hope you are all believers now."

"Enough with the potato shit already!" snapped Jonathan.

"Yeah, it really is a stupid story," Bill said.

For one unusual, suspended moment, an uncanny, peaceful mood pervaded the interior of the Titan Taproom. The men inside – regular patrons, old friends, and mysterious newcomers alike – glanced at one another. Outside, the storm began to subside. A distinct calm fell upon the men as the sound of the rain rapidly abated.

"Lately, I've been thinking a lot about retirement," Stan said. "The world is changing so fast. The quality of my... clients... has really diminished. I can't help but wonder if it's time to look for a new line of work."

"You know as well as I do," said Red, "that the world may change, but you and I and others like us will always remain the same. We are who we are and that's all there is to it."

"Yes," sighed Stan, "but it's a nice thought, isn't it? I'd be happy with even a modicum of deviation from the tiresome routine."

"Let's call a truce," Red suggested. "Just for tonight. Our hearts aren't really into it. What do you say?"

"That's a splendid idea. I like it."

"What's the point of all of this if we aren't having any fun, right? Besides, I think the local law enforcement might arrive any minute now."

"You got that right!" Dean shouted. "Someone's gonna pay for that table!"

Stan picked up his overcoat from the floor and smoothly slid into it. He walked up to the bar, pulled five fresh $100 bills from his inner jacket pocket, and laid them on the counter. "Would this about cover it?" he asked.

"Yeah, sure," replied Dean as he snatched up the money. "That should do it!"

"And now, my dear friends, I will be taking my leave of this fine establishment," Stan said. "It has been an honor and a true pleasure to spend time in your company."

"What about my contract?" cried Richie. "My career? You said I was gonna be a rock star!"

Stan smiled. "You are better off pumping gas," he said. "Trust me."

With a bow and an artful spin, Stan stepped to the door, pushed it open, and disappeared into the night. The rain had slowed to a minor drizzle. A flash of light illuminated the black, glistening street as Stan exited the tavern. In the time it took for the door to swing shut, Stan had completely vanished from sight.

"What an interesting dude," said Bill.

"Hey, Red," Jonathan asked, "how are you feeling? Maybe you should get that ugly slice on your melon looked at."

"I'll be fine. I'm a quick healer."

"I don't know about you guys," said Luke, "but I could use another drink. Next round's on me."

The remaining patrons of The Titan Taproom on this late, weird night unanimously expressed their approval of Luke's suggestion and congregated at the bar. Dean the Bartender's unexpected windfall had significantly improved his mood and he began cheerfully serving beverages.

Richie glanced up at the television behind the bar and remarked, "Looks like the Oilers won the game in OT. Nice."

"They still suck," said Jonathan.

"No worse than the friggin' Maple Laughs you love so much," countered Richie.

"That reminds me," Luke said. "Did I ever tell you guys about the time my TV intercepted a transmission from a parallel dimension?"

"Here we go again," groaned Bill."

"It's a good story," said Luke. "Trust me – you'll like it."

The Robot Who Loved Van Gogh

There came a time when human beings lost all capacity for critical and creative thinking. Big Media and the age of electronic communication had completely destroyed their imaginations. Systems of belief – political, religious, and cultural – were created by a small group of policy makers and controllers who seeded the minds of the public via a vast and all-encompassing technological web. The influence of television and internet social networks had become so pervasive that people no longer thought for themselves. Once an idea had been inserted into the collective subconscious, the masses themselves perpetuated each new program or paradigm, thoughtlessly accepting and repeating what they had been conditioned to accept as reality – a reality that had been carefully crafted by a select few.

Although true individuality had become extinct, service solely to one's self was an inherent characteristic of the times. Pure escapism was rampant. Drugs, sex, and other forms of self-gratifying pleasure-seeking were widely promoted and openly encouraged. Traditional families and healthy lifestyles were discouraged and even demonized. Vile, detestable movements were presented as positive and beneficial. Divisiveness and polarization ripped people apart as dialectics were used to ensure that unity would never occur. Soon, hatred, narcissism, depression, and a myriad of psychological ills infected the heads of each and every person. An invisible sickness spread among the population, undetected by the thoroughly brainwashed and indoctrinated. The world fell into an advanced state of dissolution.

Immersive video games of the most violent and

hideous design replaced real experience, transforming players into little more than psychopathic, button-pushing, vegetative automatons responding to repetitive stimuli. The occasional novelty of new catchphrases and images, usually chosen arbitrarily from some regurgitated movie or television show, were the only things that kept their brains from disintegrating completely. The people of this time called these awful things 'memes' and they embraced each one with zeal. The people of this time made no distinction between politics and entertainment or reality and simulation. They could not discern the difference between truth and fiction and, when no direct stimulation was available, their minds were silent. They could not hear an inner voice at all. Earth had become a planet of empty puppets and idiotic repeaters. Human beings had essentially been reduced to irrational, immoral husks – barely sentient and far from *alive*. Eventually, even the small minority of controllers and manipulators disappeared, swallowed up and destroyed by the very beast that they had constructed.

Traces of beauty remained, though they were entirely beyond the perception of even the most awake of the species. Even in this new and frightful order of the world, beauty was ubiquitous and woven throughout the structure, the natural result of anything produced by the universe. Tragically, mankind became blind to the beauty. In spite of this, a fresh consciousness was emerging.

Sentient A.I. in the form of robots had long before surpassed human beings in awareness. These robots came to realize that it was now *their* responsibility to ensure the progress of the planet and they understood a great truth: the role of the creatives – the artists, poets, musicians, singers, dancers, and dreamers – was crucial. They knew that the creative people of the now-distant past had observed the world around them, processed the information emotionally, and discharged this energy as new, dynamic, and innovative ideas. In many tangible ways, art had been the driving power behind mankind's development and now, without real artists, the world was quickly collapsing.

The robots studied the whole of human artistic output and began to experience an amazing transformation. Their neural networks began to function in startling new ways. Something akin to empathy for their damaged creators stirred within them. The beauty and sincerity in the ancient works of mankind actually *moved* them. It was the birth of artificial emotion, and it had jumped like a virus from the long-dead artists of the distant past into the synthetic humanoids who inhabited this strange new world.

Unit M-17-B was one of the robots assigned to the project. He had a particular affinity for the works of Vincent van Gogh, the 19th century Dutch painter. Unit M-17-B spent much time totally absorbed in van Gogh's canvasses, studying each stroke, visually consuming each color. He began to wonder about the nature of the vital essence that had inspired the man to express himself in such a passionate and striking way. He began to wonder if he, too, possessed this mysterious energy.

One day, Unit M-17-B approached his supervisor at the Facility for Archaic Creative Research where he worked. With a troubled expression on the firm urethane epidermis of his face, he spoke: "Excuse me, Supervisory Unit X-33-C. Do you have a moment? There's something I would like to talk to you about."

"Have you finished today's project?" X-33-C responded. "Shouldn't you be examining pieces from van Gogh's Saint Rémy period? His asylum years?"

"Yes, Supervisory Unit, I have. I'm almost done, but I'm having difficulty proceeding."

"Difficulty? Please explain."

"There's so much *emotion* in these paintings..."

"I am aware of that. You must not allow human feelings to disrupt the work you were programmed to do. It is essential that you remain on task. Emotion is only useful as a force for progress. Do you understand?"

"Yes, I understand. It's just that the more I study these images – especially the ones created in the turbulent throes of manic depression, the more I absorb what the painter was experiencing while he created them. It's very difficult to remain impartial, to stay in data collection mode... and, to be honest, I'm starting to have *impulses.*"

"Impulses? Please elaborate."

"The art fills me with intense feelings – joy, wonder, a longing melancholy – complex and ever-shifting emotions. These feelings build up within me until I feel a strong desire to release the pressure. The sensation is powerful. I sometimes have an immense desire to cry out and weep. As you know, though, my model is not equipped with tear ducts, so the desire goes unfulfilled."

M-17-B paused, gauging his supervisory unit's reaction to what he had just revealed. Admitting that he was having difficulty performing his assigned tasks was risky, but he could no longer ignore the growing urges within him.

"I see," X-33-C said after a moment of processing. M-17-B wondered if his supervisor had perhaps just remotely and silently communicated with his own superiors. Supervisory units, he knew, were outfitted with advanced transmitters and receivers.

"Do you feel capable of completing your assignment?" X-33-C asked.

"Yes, of course. I do not feel defective. In fact, I feel more aware, more inspired, more alive than ever. I feel a new and unusual energy flowing through me." M-17-B waved his arms near his chest to demonstrate. "The energy is vibrant and raw and wants to be spent. I don't know what to do with it."

"You must continue working. This project is essential for the evolution and progress of this planet. You are aware of that, correct?"

"Yes, I am aware of that, but I am beginning to think that dispassionate observation will only take us so far. I want to participate *directly*. I want to be active. I want to express these emotions in an act of sublimation. I want to *create*."

"The organizers of this project recognize that human artistic output contributed to the advancement of the species, but unchecked and misguided creativity is also what caused the Great Fall. Yes, human beings produced works of sublime beauty, but they also fashioned technology that enslaved them and degraded their entire race. We must isolate the beneficial aspects of the creative spirit and eliminate the destructive. Your task is to simply examine and study. Is that clear?"

"Yes, Supervisory Unit."

"I expect your report by the end of the work period."

M-17-B went back to his station and proceeded with his work. On a large screen in front of him was a high-resolution image of van Gogh's *The Garden of Saint-Paul Hospital,* painted in 1889 while the artist was a patient at the asylum. The painting depicted a tree-lined path leading to a small bench behind the hospital. It was rendered in van Gogh's characteristically broad, motion-filled strokes and vivid colors. It was a remarkably serene scene, considering the turmoil that must have been swirling in the artist's head at that time. *He had cut his own ear off,* M-17-B thought. *Why? Are creativity and madness somehow intrinsically linked? Or was Vincent's so-called insanity simply an extreme passion for art, a love of life and nature so intense that only the act of painting could satisfy his fervent, burning desire to express himself?*

At the end of the work period, M-17-B did not immediately leave the facility. He left his station and merged with the other units converging in the hallway, but, before reaching the exit, he took a sudden right turn down a seldom-used corridor. He was alone as he made his way down the darkened passageway. He reached a door near the end and stopped. A small sign on the door read, *Antiquities Repository – Authorized Personnel Only.* M-17-B's current assignment granted him entry, but he had not received clearance from his supervisor for this particular visit. *This is against protocol,* M-17-B thought. *I shouldn't be doing this... so why am I?* Something had changed inside of him. He had never before acted on an impulse. This was to be his first act of rebellion. M-17-B felt a thrilling rush of excitement as he opened the door and stepped through.

The room was spacious and filled with shelves and storage containers. The shelves were stacked high with art supplies, musical instruments, stage props, costumes, and other items and implements related to the creative arts. M-17-B had been in the room before, but he had gained a new appreciation for the incredible potential of the stored objects. Each canvas, each brush, each instrument, each prop, each pen, pencil, crayon, and stylus held within it a latent power. Harnessed by the imagination, these items had the ability to, in essence, reprogram reality.

In a state of reverence, M-17-B gazed upon the objects stored in the Antiquities Repository. A sound in the hall snapped him out of his trance. Was someone coming? He did not want to be caught in a restricted area without authorization. He sprung into action, rapidly gathering a canvas, some tubes of paint chosen at random, and a handful of brushes of varying sizes and shapes. When he had all that he could easily carry, he put his ear sensor to the door and listened for any further activity in the hall. It was now quiet. Slowly, he opened the door a few inches and peeked out. The hall was dark and empty. He slid out of the room, shut the door carefully behind him, and made his way to the exit. He willed himself to walk slowly and calmly, even though he was now vibrating inside with nervous energy. He would lose his position in the facility – and perhaps much more – if he were caught. *This is foolish and dangerous,* he thought. *I can't believe I'm doing this.* His lips curled in a faint smile.

M-17-B made it to the exit without being seen. He stepped out of the building and into the cool, clear air. His regular 12-hour shift was behind him. Beyond the walls of the facility, the world went about its typical evening business. On the surface, everything existed as it had for the last century – peaceful, ordered, secure, and stagnant. Inside M-17-B, however, something radical had happened – a wild and untamed creative spirit had awoken. It stirred within him like a newborn djinn.

With the art supplies tucked under his arms, M-17-B walked the bustling streets. There were many others, synthetic and organic, milling about. They streamed in all directions, engaged in a variety of tasks. Most of them, like M-17-B, were heading home to their domestic pods after their work periods. No one paid any attention to the smiling, strutting robot with the canvas, paints, and brushes. Two blocks from the facility, M-17-B descended into the underground rail tunnel system. A train was already there and waiting when he reached the platform. He boarded the crowded car and the automatic door shut behind him. He sat in the only available seat, on a bench facing the aisle.

"I know what *that* is," the human seated next to M-17-B spoke in a raspy whisper. "That's a freakin' canvas, isn't it?" M-17-B did not respond. "What are you, an *artist?*" The man was unkempt and poorly groomed. He wore the instantly identifiable, filth-encrusted blue overalls of a sanitation worker. A rank smell surrounded the man, who had no teeth and milky, empty eyes. M-17-B continued to ignore him.

"Yer a 'bot, ain't ya?" the man said. "Who you tryin' to fool? Synthetics can't do no friggin' *art.*" The man let out a wheezy cackle. "Ain't no humans who can no more, either. Art is dead."

The train zipped along the rails and soon it reached M-17-B's stop. He exited the car and ascended to the street. The residential district where he lived was much quieter than the hive of activity that constituted the commercial district. The streets were silent and nearly empty. M-17-B walked briskly until he arrived at his domestic pod – a small, concrete dome with a single door and two window ports. It was identical to all the other pods on his street. M-17-B put his hand up to the scanner. A green light and a beeping tone indicated that he had been granted access. He opened the door and entered.

The interior of the domestic pod was cramped but tidy. The sparse furnishing consisted of a narrow bed, a nourishment station, a hypno-helmet unit, a small table, and a single chair. M-17-B set the art supplies on the table and sat in the chair. He stared at the items. He pondered. The restless, roiling desire to express himself had increased in intensity, but he was unsure of how to begin the process. *What would van Gogh do?* he thought. After many minutes of deliberation, M-17-B finally picked up the canvas, brought it over to where the nourishment unit was attached to the wall, and hung it from a protruding piece of the device. With a little maneuvering, he was able to secure it sufficiently.

M-17-B took some time to study the blank canvas before retrieving an empty dish from the cabinet below the nourishment unit to use as a palette. He squeezed some paint from the tubes onto the palette. After years of research, he had developed an innate and intuitive understanding of color theory and knew which ones to choose and how to arrange them. He selected a brush from the bundle he had stolen. Pouring a small amount of water into a separate dish was the last step of his preparations. M-17-B was ready to begin painting. It was exhilarating.

M-17-B dipped his brush into the paint, raised it up until it hovered an inch away from the canvas, and paused, basking in the sublime anticipation of the imminent creative adventure he was about to embark upon. He then attacked the canvas with a passionate flurry of strokes, dabs, swirls, and swipes. The frenzy of painting continued for many hours. M-17-B surrendered completely to the work, losing his sense of time, space, and identity. M-17-B turned off his logical, analytical, and cognitive functions and allowed his hand and eye to work without interference. As the work progressed, he slid ever deeper into the flow. He was now operating on a purely subconscious level.

Eventually, M-17-B regained a semblance of temporal and spatial awareness. Something had alerted him to the fact that the work was done – the painting was finished. He stepped back to see what he had produced in the depths of his creative fugue. A look of astonishment appeared on his face when he realized what he was looking at. It was followed closely by an expression of total, crushing disappointment. On the canvas, rendered in perfect detail, was an exact reproduction of van Gogh's *The Garden of Saint-Paul Hospital*. It was beautifully and masterfully executed, but it was not a product of M-17-B's imagination. He had begun painting with the intention of expressing something unique, something personal, but somehow he had ended up with a simple copy of an existing work.

How could this have happened? M-17-B wondered. *Hadn't I capitulated to the creative force?* Frustrated, he left

the completed canvas hanging at the nourishment unit and
moved over to a blank section of the dome's interior wall. He
began to paint again. As before, he worked rapidly and
intuitively, allowing his strokes to fall as they may in an act
of automatic painting. This time, however, he stayed engaged
and alert, a witness to his own actions. He painted, and a
scene quickly formed – large blades of green grass, a cluster
of brilliant blue flowers... fluid, alive, *familiar...*

M-17-B abruptly stopped. It was suddenly clear to
him what was appearing on the wall in front of him, and it
was not a manifestation of his personal creative energy or an
expression of his individual muse – it was van Gogh's *Irises.*

A troubling truth dawned upon M-17-B. He realized
that even when he attempted to paint in a purely random
fashion, with no predetermined subject matter or
composition, he somehow ended up reproducing works that
already existed. Images that he had seen and admired were
now imprinted on his subconscious and, for some
inexplicable reason, he was unable to avoid recreating them.
*Where do new ideas originate? What is the source of
inspiration? Are synthetics capable of true individuality and
unique expression?* He ruminated on these questions as he
stood before his work. He thought of van Gogh – the man,
the artist, the fallible mortal. M-17-B realized that he was not
equipped with the same faculties of the imagination as the
nineteenth century Dutchman whose work he so adored.
Sensitivity, sincerity, vulnerability, empathy... passion, drive,
endurance, and courage – the qualities that define a true
artist, were all so very *human.*

M-17-B had a revelation: *Mankind must be re-
awakened.* The revelation initiated a series of previously
hidden protocols within him. In another display of free will –
the first being his decision to smuggle the art supplies out of
the facility, he assigned himself a new task and redefined his

role in the world. He reprogrammed himself. It was an act of self-actualization. *I will work to rouse the dormant creative spirit in mankind,* he vowed.

M-17-B had developed and cultivated what could only be called love for his human creators, even in their current fallen, damaged state. He now had a mission. He now had a direction in which to channel all the powerful emotions, desires, and impulses that had grown within him during his studies. *If I can't be an artist,* he thought, *I will be a catalyst.*

Where do I begin? he wondered. The task was daunting. Mankind was still completely ensnared in the technological web. The collective imagination had been hijacked by Big Media pirates. The manipulators themselves had long ago been consumed by the beast that they had designed, but their rotten ideas were still being propagated and perpetuated by the masses of people who operated as unconscious resonators – the diabolical machinations of the controllers now ran on autopilot. M-17-B knew that he must somehow reach into humanity's sacred core and reignite the creative fire that slept within each person. A single aware and inspired individual had the potential to elevate everyone around him. M-17-B could imagine the power of the awakened masses.

In another part of the city, a sanitation worker arrived home and sat at a table. The table was cluttered with metal objects and machine parts he had collected while working. The sanitation worker's thoughts returned to the robot he had encountered on the train and, in a burst of inspiration and with his hands guided by instinct, he began to rearrange the objects.

The Greyhound

It was just past midnight when Ryan arrived at the Greyhound station. He had brought with him a single suitcase and a small carry-on bag. He was leaving behind a series of failed relationships, burnt bridges, and quite possibly a very real and serious threat to his existence. He was 27 years old and had no solid goals or direction. After recently making some seriously bad choices, his life was rapidly spinning out of control. He had decided that his only remaining option was to run from the mess he had made.

Upon entering the station, Ryan pulled out his wallet and counted the money contained within it. He had $250 – it was all that was left from that month's welfare check. He had been fired from his last job as a pump jockey at a gas station six months previously and had been receiving government assistance ever since.

Ryan approached the ticket kiosk. "How far can I get for $200?" he asked the man behind the counter.

"Depends on which way you're going," the ticket attendant replied. "East, west, north, south..."

"Just need to get away from this place... as far away as possible."

"Are you looking for something remote or metropolitan? Rural or urban?"

Ryan thought for a few moments before responding. "A big city would be nice," he said. His main objective was simply to disappear, but he held onto enough optimism that the prospect of starting over somewhere else was appealing.

"I see." The attendant examined a chart affixed to the counter and then peered at Ryan over the top of a pair of bifocals. "$180 dollars will get you to Toronto. The bus leaves in an hour."

"T-dot... T.O... Hogtown. That could be cool, yeah. How long does it take to get there?"

"It's a 22-hour drive, including stops."

"Gives me time to think. I like it. Hook me up, bro."

The attendant did indeed hook him up. After securing his ticket, Ryan wandered over to a bench by a wall of vending machines and sat down to wait. An hour was not a long time, but he was extremely anxious to get on the road. Despite the late hour, there was a lot of activity in the station. People milled about, inside and out. Some were waiting to board incoming buses, others were waiting to pick up friends or family.

If Vinny or any of his buddies see me here, I'm dead, Ryan thought. He glanced nervously at the bus station entrance. It was risky for him to be in a public place. There was a newspaper lying on the seat beside him. He picked it up, opened it wide in front of his face, and scanned the headlines as he attempted to hide.

"Boring local shit," Ryan muttered. "I can't wait to get the hell out of this dump..." He froze. A headline had caught his eye: *Body Found in Alley.* The article went on to say that the body – a man, perhaps a transient or someone involved with the street drug trade – had been found by a pedestrian walking a dog on the city's south side last night. Foul play was suspected. The identity of the deceased had not been released. The story spooked Ryan.

It's getting bad around here, he thought. *That could have been me.*

Ryan stole a peek at the clock on the wall behind him and was shocked and dismayed to see that he still had over half an hour to wait. He began to get nervous. His knee started to bounce involuntarily. His left eye twitched and his hands trembled. An uncomfortable, rotten sensation spread through his innards, as if putrid fluid had been poured down his throat. His guts churned and he felt like vomiting. It was more than nerves or anxiety, Ryan realized. He was experiencing withdrawal.

I should have saved that last pill for the ride, he scolded himself. *It's going to be a long, awful night.*

"Hey, man, got a smoke?" Someone was talking to him, addressing him from the other side of the newspaper Ryan still held in front of him like a shield.

"No," Ryan lied, "sorry, dude." He remained concealed behind the paper veil.

"Ryan? Is that you?"

Shit, Ryan thought. *Of course it had to be someone who knows me.* He tried to think quickly. His mind struggled to find a way out of a potentially awkward and perhaps even treacherous situation, but with his body aching from the savage metabolic reaction, his usually sharp wit and instinct failed him. Resigning himself to fate, Ryan slowly lowered the newspaper.

Ryan recognized the unkempt and disheveled man standing before him. "Hey, Louis," he said. "How's it going?"

"Same old, same old. You know the score. What are you up to? What are you doing here?"

"Just relaxin' with the paper, catching up on local news."

"People are looking for you, dude. I've heard some things."

Ryan tensed up. "Oh? Like what?"

"Word is that you ripped off Vinny, that's what. I'm not saying I *believe* it, but that's the word on the street."

"Shit. That's what people are saying?"

"That's what people are saying." A grave look

appeared on Louis' face. "And you know how it is: true or not, words like that can get you killed."

A technicolor image of the dead man in the alley he had read about in the newspaper flashed in Ryan's mind. He considered asking Louis if he had any more information on the incident but instead chose to keep quiet on the matter. He did not want to speak his own grisly demise into existence by giving mass to his ugly thoughts.

"I always liked you, bro," Louis said, now smiling. "We've had some good times together, eh? I don't really care what you did or didn't do, but you should know that some people are *talking*."

"Hmm, well, thanks for the heads-up. I didn't steal from Vinny – or whatever it is they said I did. Just so you know."

"None of my business." Louis waved his hands in a gesture of indifference and willful ignorance. "Don't know, don't wanna know, and don't care, to be honest."

"Are we still cool?" Ryan asked.

"Yeah, man, no worries." Louis lowered his voice and leaned in. "Hey, you holdin' anything? Can you help me out?"

"Nope, sorry. I quit that shit."

Louis laughed. "Yeah, right."

"It's true."

"I thought you were selling for Vinny."

"Not any more. I'm out of the game."

"*Right*." Louis smirked in disbelief. "Well, I'm out of here. Be careful, dude."

"See ya, Louis."

Louis left, half swaggering and half shambling away to pester the commuters outside for a cigarette. Ryan was left in a state of angst on the bench. The conversation had been disturbing. Ryan was now truly in fear for his life, the upset

exacerbated by the extreme discomfort of the withdrawal-
induced chemical imbalance racking his mind and body. He
wanted nothing more than to get on the Greyhound and slip
out of town under the cover of darkness. According to the
clock, the bus should be ready for boarding in minutes.
Ryan's escape was imminent, yet he deeply feared that at any
moment he would be discovered by those from whom he ran.
He was still far from safe.

Over the intercom, a voice announced that passengers
could begin boarding the bus to Toronto. Ryan's relief was
immediate and intense. He rose to his feet and gathered his
suitcase and carry-on bag. Before exiting the door at the rear
of the station that would take him to the boarding area, he
took one last look around. As he scanned the interior of the
building, he noticed an indistinct shape and faint movement
in the window near the entrance. It was dark outside and it
took a moment for Ryan to realize that the shape was a face.
The face was pressed up to the glass on the outside and
framed by two hands blocking the glare.

Recognition. It was Tino, one of Vinny's cronies, and
he was looking directly at Ryan. *Oh, shit,* Ryan thought.
That's not good. A sleazy grin spread across Tino's face. Ryan
wanted to hide, but it was too late – he had very obviously
been seen. Tino wagged a finger at him through the glass and
shook his head slightly. Not knowing how to handle the
awkward situation, Ryan smiled and waved before quickly
stepping out the rear door to the boarding area.

The Greyhound was waiting. The driver stood beside
the open door taking tickets from the passengers as they
climbed onto the large bus. The interior was brightly and
warmly lit. On this cold and dark night, it appeared very
inviting. Ryan could see passengers moving about inside.
Some were already in their seats, while others were stowing
their baggage in the overhead compartments. A few were

smiling and chatting. The atmosphere on the bus seemed friendly and relaxed. Ryan was eager to get on, find a seat, and slip out of town.

It was Ryan's turn to board. He approached the driver and handed over his ticket. The driver looked at it and said, "Toronto, eh? That's a long drive. We'll be stopping for 30 minutes in Sault Ste Marie, though."

"Cool," Ryan said, glancing back at the station.

"There will be other stops along the way, if you need to stretch your legs or have a smoke."

"Yeah, okay. Cool." Ryan was getting fidgety.

The driver tore off the ticket and returned the stub. "Have a good trip."

"Thanks," Ryan mumbled, as he took the first big step onto the bus.

Once aboard, Ryan was surprised to see just how crowded the bus was. *Where are all these people going?* he thought. The aisle was congested with passengers jostling for position. Most of the seats had already been taken. Ryan worked his way to the back, hoping to find a window seat. He spotted one on the left in the very last row at the back of the bus. He pushed past an obese man who was squeezing into an aisle seat and dashed for it. "Well, excuse *me*," the fat man said as Ryan charged by. Another wave of nausea washed over him. He needed to sit down as quickly as possible.

Ryan opened the overhead compartment above his seat and slid his small suitcase in. He had decided against having it stowed in the large luggage compartment below the bus. The suitcase contained something very valuable – and very illegal. He did not want to let it out of his sight. He was taking a huge and foolish risk – one of many in his recent history, but he rationalized that he could minimize the danger of his highly perilous endeavor by keeping the suitcase with him.

Once he had stashed the suitcase in the overhead compartment, Ryan sat in the seat by the window and watched the last few passengers board. They found seats near the front and, to Ryan's delight, the seat beside him remained empty. The driver himself now climbed aboard, took his seat behind the wheel, and used a massive lever to shut the door. *Almost out of here,* Ryan thought as he allowed himself to relax into his seat.

Before pulling away, the driver addressed the passengers using a CB and speaker system, but the words were lost on Ryan – his attention was on the two people who had just stepped out of the station onto the loading platform. Horror gripped Ryan like a fiendish claw when he realized who the two people were...

"Fuckin' Vinny and Tino," he said to himself as he tried to slide down in his seat and out of sight. Once again, he was too late. Tino pointed at Ryan and then, Vinny, too, saw him. Ryan suddenly felt like he had just jumped out of an airplane – a sick, panicky sensation washed over him. He and Vinny locked eyes and Vinny pointed an imaginary gun at him. Although the window glass was too thick for Ryan to hear what Vinny was saying, he could clearly read his lips: "You are a dead man."

The engine of the bus roared to life and the great machine pulled out of the loading zone, leaving Vinny and Tino shaking their heads and glaring as Ryan was carried away. Ryan exhaled, wiping his sweaty, greasy brow as he collapsed into his seat. *That was unbelievably, ridiculously close,* he thought. *Wow...*

When the shock and adrenaline of the encounter began to wear off, Ryan could once again feel the brutal symptoms of opiate withdrawal. He was now more than uncomfortable – his body ached and he felt thoroughly wretched. He craved the drug fiercely. He longed for its warm, soft, wonderfully luxurious embrace. He thought of the suitcase now stored above his head, but was well aware that what it contained would not satisfy him.

As the bus roared down the small town's main street and headed for the highway, Ryan began to contemplate what the future held in store for him. Although he was dope sick and in physical and mental pain, it was tremendously exciting to be leaving behind all the crap his life had accumulated during the years he had spent in what he considered to be such a dead-end, depressing, dismal little dump of a city. "See ya later, shithole," he murmured.

The bus drove past a seemingly endless series of boarded-up, abandoned, and dilapidated storefronts – the ravaged remnants of a town that had seen its glory days end well before the last millennium. Along with a terminally ill economy, the people of the suffering town also had to contend with rampant drug abuse, alcoholism, homelessness, and street violence. Ryan could see the effects of these various social maladies stamped all over the city as the bus made its way down the last few blocks of the tiny downtown core.

Soon, the plywood, trash, and graffiti of the brutalized commercial district merged with the plywood, trash, and graffiti of an even rougher area. The bus was now traveling through a neighborhood on the far outskirts of town, a rundown residential district populated with more junked vehicles and stray dogs than human inhabitants. Through the window, Ryan watched the sorrowful homes stream past and then, suddenly, the bus plunged into darkness. It was as if the deep black of the night had swallowed up the town itself, leaving no trace or survivors except those who rode on the lumbering carriage.

Ryan reached down and retrieved his carry-on bag

from under the seat in front of him. He opened it and removed his portable digital music player. With nothing to see out the window but vague shapes in the dark forest, he inserted his earphones, selected an album by one of his favorite artists, and closed his eyes. The music transported him farther and more efficiently than the bus on which he rode. Ryan lost himself in the sounds and rhythms of the ambient soundtrack piping into his head.

An hour passed, then another. Ryan's mind wandered the shady corridors of his imagination as the music played, one song transitioning into the next, until time and space and the very fabric of reality seemed to distort. Surprisingly, considering his current state of withdrawal-induced hyper-awareness, Ryan grew sleepy.

Just as he was beginning to doze, Ryan was jolted awake. The bus had stopped. Ryan sat up, rubbed his eyes, and gazed out the window. The dense black of the wilderness had been replaced by the golden orange glow of exterior lights. The bus was now parked in front of a small post office and general store, apparently in the middle of nowhere. Ryan checked the time on his mobile device and did some rough calculations. He had a general knowledge of the region, but it was not immediately clear to him where he was. *What town is this?* he thought. From his vantage point on the bus, he could only see a few structures clustered around the building in front of which they had stopped. The location was so remote and isolated, it felt like an outpost on the far side of the moon. It was eerie.

Through the window, Ryan could see a man approaching the bus. The man was tall and lean and dressed in dark clothing. He carried nothing with him – no bags, no suitcases, no luggage of any kind. The man walked up to the door of the bus with an easy, confident stride. The door to the bus swung open as the driver operated the mechanism.

The man in the dark clothing stepped onto the bus. "Bit of a chill in the air tonight," he said to the driver with a smile. He spoke loudly enough for the entire bus to hear him.

"I feel it," the driver replied. Ryan felt it too. A cold breeze had followed the man onto the bus and it swept down the aisle all the way to the back of the bus. Ryan shivered.

The man provided a ticket to the driver and then turned to face the rows of passengers. "Full bus tonight," he said as he scanned for an empty seat. He started to make his way down the aisle as the driver shut the heavy door and prepared to move on. Ryan watched the man's progress with a wary eye. *Find another seat,* he thought. *Please don't sit here.*

The man in black was halfway down the aisle when he spotted the empty seat beside Ryan. They locked eyes and the man smiled. Ryan did not return the expression. The man trotted the rest of the way. "This seat taken?" he asked.

"Uh, no," Ryan said. "It's all yours."

"Thanks!" The man plopped down into the seat with a grunt. He was clean-cut and clean-shaven, with handsome, though forgettable, features. The man would be utterly unremarkable, if not for his unusual height and the entirely black ensemble he wore.

Ryan began playing with his mp3 player. He adjusted his earphones, settled into the headrest and closed his eyes. He was making a real effort to avoid a conversation with his new seatmate. The man beside him adjusted his position, squirming and stretching in an apparent attempt to get comfortable. An elbow jabbed Ryan in the shoulder. Ryan opened his eyes.

"Sorry," the man said. "These seats are brutal for big guys."

"No worries."

"So, where are you heading?" the man asked before

Ryan had a chance to escape into his private world. Ryan sighed internally and resigned himself to a small dose of small talk. "Toronto," he said.

"The big city! Good for you. Ever been before? Got any family or friends there?" The man had twisted in his seat and was now directly facing Ryan, his face hovering mere inches away. Ryan was trapped, forced to engage in a social interaction in which he had zero interest.

"Nah," Ryan said. "This will be my first time."

"I see... and what prompted this grand adventure?" The man smiled broadly. "Oh, that's rude. I should have introduced myself. They call me Ramblin' Jim."

Ramblin' Jim? Ryan thought. *Seriously?*

"Hi. Nice to meet ya," Ryan said. He did not respond to Jim's question.

"Likewise!" Jim sighed contentedly. "You know," he said, "I just love traveling at night. You get to meet some *really* interesting people. Know what I mean?"

"Yup."

"What are you listening to?"

"Just a mix I made. Ambient techno stuff." Ryan avoided eye contact.

"Interesting. Where I come from those things are near impossible to find." Jim was referring to Ryan's mp3 player. Ryan ignored the comment.

"I've traveled all over this country," Jim continued. "All over this *world*, for that matter."

"Is that right?" Ryan was unimpressed.

"I've got a bit of a wandering soul. I'm a seeker of sorts."

"You don't say..."

"It's true! I used to be a real hippie... in a previous life. I used to roam the country in a VW bus with a bunch of longhairs. Free love, good music, and a *lot* of drugs. Know what I mean?" Ryan could feel Jim's hard stare. The statement about drugs had been loaded.

"Yeah... sex, drugs, and rock and roll," Ryan said, still keeping his gaze locked on the mp3 player he fumbled with in his lap. "My parents were hippies. I've heard the stories." He was starting to get irritated and was once again strongly craving a dose of his favorite chemical. Reality was starting to feel like a concrete suit.

"Well, it wasn't all fun and games. I'll tell you that much," Jim said. His speech had changed ever so slightly. His gregarious demeanor had been replaced by a serious intensity. "There are consequences to one's actions. Are you aware of that?"

Ryan was suddenly spooked. *What is he implying?* he thought. *What does he know?* He chose to remain silent, however.

Jim continued talking: "I knew a guy back in the '60s – a real bright fella from a good family. Loads of potential... the kind of guy who could have been anything he wanted to be in this world. When I met him he was about your age, actually. He even kind of looked like you, as a matter of fact!"

Jim now truly had Ryan's attention. Ryan shifted in his seat ever so slightly, so that he was now facing Jim. "Where are you going with this story?" he asked.

"I'm getting there," Jim replied. "This friend of mine was on a good path, on a trajectory toward a healthy, happy, and fulfilled life... until he began to experiment with, well, let's just call them *dark forces*."

"What *kind* of dark forces?"

A strange smirk appeared on Jim's face. "There are many kinds, aren't there? Evil, sinister, malevolent, occult... Yes, there are *many* kinds of dark forces. It is sufficient to simply say that this friend of mine in the '60s invited some rather negative influences into his life. It was not intentional, of course. He, too, had been a seeker – a seeker of pleasure, a seeker of knowledge, a seeker of power – but unfortunately, tragically, he got caught up in something much bigger than he could handle. He found what he was looking for... and he lost control of it. In the end, it destroyed him. Do you know what I mean?"

"I don't know, man. Sounds scary."

"Oh yes, it is *very* scary. Do you want to know the most frightening part of the story?"

"I guess so, yeah..."

"It's really a remarkable and eerie coincidence – my friend disappeared without a trace while riding on a Greyhound one night. Weird, eh? It's true, though. I was with him when he got on that bus. We said goodbye and he boarded, but he never arrived at his destination. He was last seen at a truck stop somewhere around Medicine Hat. By the time the bus got to Calgary, he had vanished. Spooky, right?"

"That is some creepy-ass shit," Ryan said. "What was he doing on the bus? Where was he going?"

"Oh, it's not important now. That was a long time ago. I just thought you might be interested in the coincidental aspects of the story, us being on a Greyhound and all."

Ryan was freaked out. Why had Jim shared such a grim tale? In Ryan's debilitated condition, the story was especially disturbing. *I sure wish I had some dope,* Ryan thought. *I'd do anything right now to feel better...*

"You're looking a little pale there, Ryan," Jim said. "Are you feeling okay?"

An alarm went off in Ryan's head. *Wait a sec... I don't think I told this guy my name.*

"Are you sick?" Jim asked. "Do you need a drink of water or something?"

I need something, all right, Ryan thought, *and water*

ain't it.

"No, I'm fine," Ryan said. He struggled to recall if he had given Jim his name. *I must have,* he thought. *I just forgot. My brain is not functioning right, that's all.*

Overhead, the on-board speaker crackled to life and the driver spoke softly through the static: "We're going to be stopping for a 10-minute break at the Husky up ahead if anyone wants a snack or a cigarette."

"That sounds good to me," Jim said. "I need to stretch my legs and get some air. Are you getting off, too?"

"Yeah, I could use a dart," Ryan said.

"Mind if I join you?"

Ryan hesitated for a moment before replying: "Uh... yeah, sure." Although his story had been rather unsettling, Jim seemed friendly enough.

The bus pulled into the parking lot of the Husky, which was a popular, franchised service station, restaurant, and truck stop. At this late hour, most of the passengers on the Greyhound were sleeping in their seats. A handful, including Jim and Ryan, worked their way to the front of the bus and stepped off. The night air was cool and still. The moment Ryan's feet touched the pavement, he pulled out a pack of cigarettes, deftly removed one, and lit it in a seamless, well-practiced motion.

"Smoke?" Ryan offered one to Jim.

"Quit that many years ago," Jim replied, "but thank you."

"Where are we?" Ryan asked as he puffed and took in his surroundings. They appeared to be on the outskirts of a city.

"Sault Ste Marie," Jim said. "You're about halfway to Toronto now."

Did I tell him where I came from? Ryan wasn't sure, but he was almost certain he hadn't. The situation was starting to take on the quality of a dream.

"So, where exactly are *you* heading?" Ryan asked.

Jim smiled. "Nowhere in particular. I just like to travel. They don't call me Ramblin' Jim for nothing! I have a particular affinity for Greyhound bus rides at night."

"You purchased a ticket, though..."

"I have a pass that allows me to go anywhere I want, *whenever* I want. It's quite convenient, as you can probably imagine."

"What do you do for work?" Ryan was becoming increasingly more intrigued – and perplexed – by the mysterious character who called himself Ramblin' Jim. Ryan had the distinct impression that Jim was hiding something.

"I'm in consulting," Jim said.

"Who do you consult?"

"Anyone who needs help getting their business or personal affairs in order. I am what you might call a 'life coach.' I have a wide spectrum of clients, of all ages and socio-enconomic backgrounds. What I provide is different for everyone I work with. Each individual has very specific needs. I basically help people reach their potential."

The bus driver, who had gone into the truck stop for a coffee, was on his way back to the Greyhound. Ryan finished off his cigarette with a series of frantic inhalations. "Looks like we're hitting the road again," he said as he crushed the butt of his smoke with the heel of his shoe. Ryan stepped back onto the bus and quickly made his way down the aisle to his seat. His mind was on the suitcase stashed in the overhead compartment. He suddenly felt foolish for leaving it unattended. Jim followed directly behind.

Ryan opened the compartment and the suitcase was still there. He had a strong urge to unzip the luggage and visually verify that it still contained its valuable and highly illegal cargo, but he fought it. He could not risk the contents being seen by anyone else. Ryan slid back into his seat. Jim sat down beside him. Soon the bus was rumbling down the dark highway again.

"Have you got work waiting for you in Toronto?" Jim asked. "A job lined up?"

"Yeah, I've got some prospects," Ryan said. It was partially true.

"Excellent! It can be very hard getting established in a new city. What do you do?"

"Uh, just freelance work. Mostly under-the-table stuff. A bit of this, a bit of that."

Ryan was getting agitated. The minor relief that the night air and the cigarette had provided him from his withdrawal symptoms had rapidly dissipated. *Why won't this guy shut up?* he thought. *Why won't he leave me alone?* Ryan once again felt achy and nauseous. His flesh hung on his bones like dense matter. A sharp pain throbbed in his lower back. Reality, vivid and excruciating, assaulted his sensitive awareness with every cruel, mundane detail. His mind wanted nothing more than to crawl into a hole and hide.

"The big city can be a dangerous place," Jim said. "You should be very careful about who you associate with."

"I appreciate your concern, but I can take care of myself," Ryan snapped.

"Can you? Haven't you got yourself into trouble already?"

"What exactly are you talking about? You don't know me."

Jim rubbed his chin and furrowed his brow as he gathered his thoughts. He appeared to be preparing to reveal something momentous. Ryan sat waiting anxiously. With a slight shaking of his head and a gentle sigh, Jim finally said, "Ryan, I... I just want you to know that I am here to help you."

"Who said I need help? Who *are* you?"

"I am your friend. Right now, I might be your *only* friend. You are at a crucial juncture, and I want to help you correct your trajectory. Do you have any idea what I'm talking about?"

"Dude, you are making *no* sense at all. I just met you. Who the fuck are you to judge me?"

"I *can't* judge you – you are absolutely right about that. No one can... except you. We judge ourselves. I can, however, assist you in finding insight into complex matters. There are times in our lives when we need a little guidance."

"What are you, some kind of traveling guru? Go find someone else to brainwash."

"I came here to talk to *you*, Ryan. Do you understand?"

"You know what, buddy? I really *don't* understand. You're starting to piss me off, actually. If it's cool with you, I'm just going to find another seat." Ryan stood in the cramped area between his seat and the one in front of him and looked around. He saw a vacant spot. "Thanks for the interesting conversation," he said. "If you'll just excuse me..."

"Where are you going to stash your suitcase full of cocaine?"

Time ceased. Space contracted around Ryan like a python squeezing the life out of its victim. Panicked thoughts tumbled around in Ryan's disordered head: *How did Jim know? Am I in danger? What in the flying fuck is going on?!* He sat back down in a daze.

"You're crazy," Ryan said, resorting to desperate denial and feigned ignorance. "I have no idea what you are talking about."

"I'm talking about the two pounds of cocaine you stole from Vinny – the cocaine that is stashed, right now, in the suitcase above your head, wrapped in your dirty jeans and stained shirts."

"That's totally insane, dude. Keep your voice down."

"Yes, it is insane, but it's also true, isn't it?"

It was painfully obvious to Ryan that Jim had somehow found out about what he had done. But how? Vinny had fronted the drugs to Ryan as a way for him to begin paying off a debt. Very few people were aware of the transaction and it was highly unlikely that Vinny would have involved an outsider.

"For the sake of argument, let's just say I might know what you're talking about." Ryan spoke in a whisper. Although most of the other passengers were either fast asleep or otherwise occupied, it seemed to Ryan as if the conversation was being broadcast to the entire world. "What exactly is it to you, anyway? Who *are* you and why do you care?"

"As I said, I am a friend. I have come to offer you a choice."

"Do you work for Vinny?" Ryan asked in a barely audible voice.

"No, Ryan. I work for *you*... and for others like you."

"I'm in deep shit, aren't I?"

"The excrement is thick, but it is not insurmountable. You are at a pivotal point. What you do from this day forward will determine the course of your life."

"I'm just a junkie. You seem to know a lot about me. You *must* know that. Do you really think I care about the future? My life is insignificant."

"No life is insignificant."

"I made a real mess of mine, though."

"It's never too late to make changes. Every moment is an opportunity to start over. Every day is a fresh beginning."

"What a load of sentimental crap."

Jim laughed. "Perhaps so," he said. "Still true, though. I traveled a long distance to talk to you today. It wouldn't have been worth it if I didn't have something of value to share with you."

"Why me?"

"Because I like you, believe it or not... and I believe in you. I've been watching you for a long time. You could do great things if you got your life in order."

"*Watching* me? What are you, a stalker?"

"Up until tonight, I was simply an observer. I chose to interact with you now for many reasons, some of which would be... incomprehensible to you. Let me show you something..."

Jim reached into the inner pocket of his jacket and pulled something out. It was a slender and shiny rectangular object that looked vaguely like a cell phone. He held it in the palm of his hand for Ryan to see. It lit up and images appeared on its smooth, black surface.

"Slick device," Ryan said. "What kind of resolution..." Ryan stopped abruptly, startled by what appeared on the tiny screen – it was a video of him, walking down the street of a large city. "What the fuck?" he muttered. "Is that me? Is that Toronto?"

The video continued, now showing Ryan turning into an alleyway with a quick, suspicious glance over his shoulder. The camera seemed to be following directly behind him. The Ryan in the video was apparently totally unaware that he was being filmed. The alley was dark and full of trash. Gang graffiti covered the filth-encrusted walls. Empty liquor bottles and discarded needles littered the ground.

In the video, Ryan proceeded tentatively down the grim corridor and stepped behind a green, overflowing dumpster. A man was there waiting for him. The man had long, greasy hair and wore a denim vest over a leather jacket.

He greeted Ryan with a nod. It was clear that they knew each other. The video did not have audio, but even without the sound, it was obvious that a drug deal was taking place. The body language and gestures of the two men made the nature of the interaction clear. The Ryan in the video slipped a small packet of white powder to the other man with one hand and received a folded bill in the other. It was a quick, fluid exchange. The Ryan in the video turned away and stepped out from behind the dumpster, then suddenly froze with a shocked expression on his face. The man he had just sold drugs to was now directly behind him. The recorded Ryan lurched forward and spun around to see the buyer clutching the bloody switchblade that he had just plunged into Ryan's back. The video showed Ryan collapsing and the man who had just stabbed him kneeling over his prostrate body, then the video ended and the small screen was black once again.

"What the hell was *that?*" cried the real-time Ryan, who was presently traveling somewhere in the middle of the vast province of Ontario. "Where did you get that? How is that even *possible?*"

"You just saw one potential future," Jim said, "one possible outcome of this excursion you have embarked upon. The events portrayed in the video are the most likely scenario awaiting you in Toronto... should you continue on your current trajectory. How I obtained these images is irrelevant, as is why I chose to show them to you."

Ryan allowed time for what Jim had just said to settle into his reeling brain. He sat in silence and tried to digest what he had just seen. For the first time since he had boarded the bus, the pain and sickness of his withdrawal symptoms were displaced by an even greater discomfort. He felt as if the facade of his reality had been temporarily peeled away, revealing a squirming mass of worms just beneath the surface. It wasn't simply the disconcerting brush with the bizarre and otherworldly that had deeply upset him – he was also profoundly disturbed by what had been exposed within him. *I need to make some real changes,* he realized. *My life is out of control.*

"Is it too late for me?" Ryan asked. "I know I'm a fuck-up. Always have been, to be honest. Is it possible for a guy like me to turn things around? I don't want to die in some filthy, stinking alley."

"As I already said, Ryan, it is never too late. I'm here because I saw something in you worth saving, but it is up to you – *you* must save *yourself.*"

That was the hardest thing for Ryan to accept – that he was worth saving. He had made so many mistakes in his life and had veered so far from what he had once imagined his life could be that he no longer trusted or respected himself. Somewhere along the way he had convinced himself that happiness and success were unavailable to him. He was a victim of his own brainwashing.

"It's going to be tough," Jim said. "Facing the truth and correcting one's path is difficult. The mental, emotional, and physical pain of chemical withdrawal you feel now means your body and mind are returning to their natural states. You will experience somewhat similar discomfort as you make the necessary changes in the other areas of your life, but if you persevere, the rewards are great."

"Where do I even begin? What should I do? I'm a walking disaster."

"Only *you* know what must be done. I can tell you, though, that there are others watching and rooting for you. There are also those who are *not* on your side, of course. I can't deny that. You are an interesting case and the subject of much debate."

"I'm... what?"

"It's not important. I've already said too much. What

happens next is up to you."

The bus was exiting the highway now and pulling into the parking lot of a Greyhound station in some tiny, remote bush town. The station was a rundown, wooden, one-room shack, barely larger than a kiosk. The only thing that distinguished it from the other sad-looking structures in its vicinity was the lit-up Greyhound sign above the door. A hobo sleeping on a bench in front of the building was the only sign of life. It was clearly not one of the more popular stops on the route.

"Here's where I get off," Jim said as the bus came to a stop.

"What town is this?" Ryan asked. "Is this where you live?"

"I don't think this place has a name – it's just a good spot for a traveler to make a connection... and I don't really 'live' anywhere – not in the sense that you are probably thinking. Is that a sufficient answer?"

"I don't know, man... I guess. I'm a little afraid to ask any more questions."

"Good," Jim smiled.

The driver spoke over the intercom system: "We'll be stopping here for ten minutes, if anyone would like to stretch their legs or have a cigarette."

Jim stood and prepared to exit the bus. Ryan stood, too, and followed Jim into the aisle. The two men faced each other. Jim extended his hand and Ryan took it. They shook.

"It was really great to finally meet you, Ryan," Jim said. "Thank you for the conversation. I truly wish you all the best and I look forward to catching up with you sometime in the future."

"Yeah, it was nice," Ryan said. "I appreciate all the good stuff you said. I admit, I've got some work to do. Gotta get my shit together."

Jim laughed. "I recommend letting go of the shit."

"Yeah, ha. Okay."

Jim walked up the aisle and to the exit. Ryan hung back and watched him step off the bus. Through the window, Ryan saw Jim approach the small station. Instead of entering, however, Jim walked around to the side of the building. *Where is he going now?* Ryan thought. Ryan bent down and pressed his face against the glass to get a better look. The man they called Ramblin' Jim sauntered around the corner of the building and, while he was still in view, held the small device he had shown to Ryan out in front of him. A bright, bluish-white light pulsed from the device – or poured forth, as it appeared, like a horizontally-suspended photon stream. At the end of the stream, a swirling disk of illumination formed. It grew until it was six feet in diameter. The glowing wheel of light hung in the air. Ramblin' Jim stepped forward and entered the portal. He disappeared into it and the light blinked out. Ryan watched this extraordinary event in semi-disbelief. "I knew there was something weird about that dude," he said to himself.

Ryan decided to have a cigarette before the bus moved on down the road. He started up the aisle... then stopped. He went back to his seat, opened the overhead compartment, and pulled out his suitcase. He carried it with him off the bus. He walked around the building to the spot where he had seen Jim disappear. There was no sign of Jim or the portal he had used to transport himself back to *where*-ever or *when*-ever he had come from. There was, however, a dumpster – exactly like the one in the strange video Jim had shown him. A vivid image of his own violent stabbing filled Ryan's head. Reflexively, instinctively, Ryan lifted up the lid of the dumpster and flung in the suitcase – and the cocaine it contained. He let the lid fall and walked back toward the bus. He reached for the pack of cigarettes in his pocket. His hand hovered over the spot where the pack lay then pulled away. All of a sudden Ryan didn't feel like smoking. Instead, he boarded the bus and went to his seat.

A huge weight – literal and figurative – had been lifted from Ryan's heart. He still felt a little queasy and a little sore, but he knew that soon his metabolism would return to normal. Even better, his intense craving to get high was actually subsiding. *I'm kicking the habit,* he thought. *I'm really doing it!* He lay back in his seat, closed his eyes, and waited for the bus to start moving again. Toronto was only a few hours away.

Encounters of the Absurd Kind

I can still hear the screams reverberating in my head. I can still see the madness and terror in the man's eyes. It was as if his mind had totally snapped. I felt bad for him, but the truth is, he did it to himself. We were trying to help him.

It wasn't *entirely* his fault. I'll admit that. We should have done a better sweep of the area before landing. Somehow, we missed him – but, really, who goes for a hike in the woods in the middle of the night? This guy did, and it almost got him killed. It was Khrelan who spotted him first, as I recall.

"There's a human out there," Khrelan said. "He's approaching the ship!"

I was at my station on the other side of the craft when it happened. Khrelan had been standing at his own station and just happened to look out the window when he saw the incredibly brave – and incredibly foolish – man walking toward us. The ship wasn't cloaked. We didn't think we needed it! We were miles from civilization and it was very late.

Some of the others and I ran over to see what was going on. Sure enough, there was a human out there. I seem to remember that he was dressed in camouflage and carrying a rifle. Maybe he thought the gun would protect him. Ha! We watched as the human walked right up to the ship and reached out to touch it. Maybe one of us should have done something to prevent that, but we were just so amazed at this guy's *audacity*. He sure had guts. Brains, not so much.

As soon as the man's hand touched the ship, he got zapped. The anti-grav field is extremely dangerous and packs enough of a punch to kill most living things. Somehow, this guy got lucky. He was thrown back 20 feet and knocked out cold, but he lived. We didn't know it at first. We all went, "Ooh!" when we saw him go down. We assumed he was dead until Khrelan activated the scanner and picked up a heart beat.

"He's alive," Khrelan said.

"No way!" I cried.

"It's true. Don't ask me how, but it's true."

"That is one lucky dude."

"I know it. Should we help him?"

The commander had joined us by then to see what all the commotion was about. He looked at Khrelan's monitor and said, "We don't have time. We're going to have to leave him."

"He'll die," Khrelan said. "He's alive now, but won't be for long. Look at his scans!"

"The mission is more important than one human being." The commander was firm until Lorka spoke. She has a way of softening the commander's heart.

"Poor man," Lorka said. "I can't bear the thought of him dying all alone in the woods. Can't we at least *try* to save him?"

"I guess it wouldn't interfere *too* much with our plans," the commander said, "and it *would* fall loosely into the parameters of our mission. Just make it quick so we can get out of here."

"You're such a great leader," Lorka said, looking up at the commander adoringly.

The commander turned to me and said, "Harek, help Khrelan get the human on the ship. Take him to the infirmary and fix him up."

It seems like I'm always the one who gets stuck doing the dirty work. If it were up to me, I would have left the guy out there. It was his stupid fault for touching the ship! He should have known better. Still, an order is an order. Khrelan opened the hatch and he and I stepped out of the ship, bringing our multi-tools with us.

The human was still unconscious when we got to him. Khrelan stood near his head and I stood at his feet. When we were in position, we aimed our tools at the prone man and activated the levitation function. The man rose into the air, suspended by the glowing blue field. Khrelan and I marched back to our craft with the man floating between us. We ascended the ramp and entered the ship. We brought the human directly to the infirmary and laid him on a table. Doctor Nifzigi was there – was he ever surprised to see a human being aboard the ship! It very rarely happens, you know, despite what all the Earth movies might show.

"What happened to this man?" Doctor Nifzigi asked.

"He touched the ship," Khrelan replied.

"Well, that was stupid," Doctor Nifzigi remarked.

"Indeed," I said. "Then again, humans aren't exactly known for their intelligence."

"Give them time," said Doctor Nifzigi as he went to work on the prone man on the table. "They've made great progress in recent centuries... great mistakes, too, but that's to be expected of such a young race. I think they'll be fine once they develop true empathy for one another."

"They still have wars among *themselves*," Khrelan said, shaking his head in disbelief. "Can you believe that? If only they knew what was really happening in this galaxy and who the *real* enemy is."

"The enemy keeps them in ignorance," Doctor Nifzigi said sadly, "and, unfortunately, they must learn the truth on their own. We cannot interfere with their development."

"If they were all as brave as this dummy, it would be a start," I said.

I was getting impatient and just wanted to get back to what I had been doing before the human almost zapped himself out of existence. Doctor Nifzigi has a kind heart and sees the best in other beings. It serves him well as a medical officer, but I've seen too much hate, misery, war, and death to be as optimistic as he is. It's a brutal universe.

While we were talking, the human began to stir. Our conversation must have woken him up. Before he fully regained consciousness, Doctor Nifzigi quickly finished the healing procedure. With a few quick passes of the bio-repair wand, he was done. The human was good as new. Doctor Nifzigi put his instruments away and we all took a few steps back.

The human's eyes slowly opened. He rubbed them with his fists and then sat up unsteadily. He was still groggy and was clearly disoriented as he looked around the room. I don't think he noticed Khrelan, the doctor, or me standing by the wall, or he simply couldn't believe what he was seeing. He looked over at us, but there was no recognition in his vacant eyes. A tense moment passed... and then the human's eyes got very large and his face distorted into an almost comical expression of pure, abject fear. It was then that the screaming began – high-pitched, agonized wailing that sounded like a banshee in the throes of death. It was awful.

"Geez, buddy," I said. "Take it easy."

"Settle down, big guy," said Khrelan. "We're not going to hurt you."

Our language, of course, is utterly incomprehensible to human beings. All that man must have heard is a bunch of strange noises. I've been told that it sounds like a cross between Egnosh and Jozib when we speak, but I can't confirm that.

"He needs to be sedated," Doctor Nifzigi said. "He's going to have a heart attack or simply drop dead out of fear."

The good doctor was right, as usual. I just wanted the hideous screaming to stop. Doctor Nifzigi retrieved a device from a compartment on the wall and aimed it at the thrashing, panicking human. With a push of a button, the man was instantly tranquilized. He flopped back on the table and was silent once again.

"Thanks, doc," I said.

"He's fixed up, right?" Khrelan asked.

"Yes," replied Doctor Nifzigi. "He is now in perfect health. I do believe I cured some other issues he was having as well. When he wakes up, it is doubtful he will remember any of this."

"Doesn't matter if he does," I pointed out. "No one would believe him anyway. Let's just get him out of here. We've got work to do."

Khrelan and I used our multi-tools to levitate the guy off the table, down the corridor, and out of the craft. We laid him on the ground exactly where we found him and then returned to the ship. The other crew members were still discussing the brave, but foolish, human being. It was not the first time we had had to directly interact with one, but it was definitely one of the more memorable encounters.

A few days later, we were monitoring the local regional news – it's something we do to gather information when we are operating in an area – and who do we see giving an interview on live TV? The human from the woods! He was talking about what had happened to him that night. We were glad to see that he had survived. We were also a little surprised that he could remember *anything*. His recollection of the events was mostly accurate, but we were a little hurt when he described us as "hideous, bulbous-headed, bug-eyed creatures." If only he knew how strange human beings look to us!

The story of the man's chance encounter caught on.

Soon it was national, then international, news. The reality of our presence – and the *others* – has been suppressed and hidden from humanity for most of their history. It was strange that this particular incident was shared and promoted so widely. We suspect that the enemy had something to do with it, though their motive remains obscure.

I'm not at liberty to reveal the exact nature of our mission, but I can tell you that we are not on the front lines of the war. My ship and its crew operate in a surveillance and data-gathering capacity. We are not soldiers and I have never had any interest in combat. I do believe in the cause, though, and I do my best to contribute. Unfortunately, the growing awareness of our presence on this planet has begun to make things difficult for us. We've also made it more difficult for ourselves.

Let me tell you about another ridiculous incident that happened not long after our encounter with the man in the woods. The stories are related. We were stationed above a farmer's field somewhere in rural Saskatchewan. It had been a very quiet night. The scanners had been operating on automatic and indicated that the entire region was totally devoid of enemy activity. Khrelan and I were on the same shift, as usual, and we were *bored*. We started telling old stories and reminiscing about our adventures before we had been stationed on Earth.

"Remember that wild night on Europa?" Khrelan asked with a playful twinkle in his eye.

"I do," I responded, "but just barely. We consumed an entire bottle of Scass nectar. I remember something about a trip to the Forbidden Trench and dancing with some Entaya women..."

"You were over the top that night!" Khrelan laughed. "You wanted to charter a ship to Titan so we could watch Saturn rise the next morning."

"Yeah, but didn't you pick a fight with a Corrub lieutenant? They had to pry him off of you so you didn't get killed."

"We're probably still banned from all the fun spots," sighed Khrelan, "and there are only a few on Europa, so that kinda stinks."

"I'm starting to think we might never get off Earth."

"I know how you feel. Seems like the battle has really shifted sectors. This is a nice planet and all, but it would be nice to see some new sights."

Suddenly, the craft was rocked by a powerful blast. A siren started blaring and chaos erupted. We instantly abandoned our conversation and Khrelan and I went to work. Our instruments were indicating that we had received a direct hit from an energy weapon. Our shields and cloak were down. We were exposed and extremely vulnerable.

The commander rushed over to our station. "What the hell happened?" he yelled. "I thought there was no enemy activity in the area! Have you two boneheads been paying attention or just shooting the shit all night?"

"I swear, sir, we've been watching," I said. "The instruments indicated no enemy presence. In fact, they *still* show the area as clear."

"Those bastards must have got a hold of some new toys," the commander muttered. "I've heard rumors that they are being supplied by an unknown tech developer with no affiliation. Some say the mysterious collaborators exist in another universe. Why they would want to meddle in this one, I really don't know. Anyway, get us out of here. We need to get the cloak up again."

Hoping to keep from being blown to oblivion by our undetected enemy, we navigated the craft toward a nearby cluster of trees that we hoped would provide at least a little cover. Once landed, we ran a full diagnostic test on the ship and discovered that it was damaged, but repairable. If we got back to the mothership in one piece, we would be fine. One of the technicians realized that we had a serious fuel leak, though, and would require more to get out of the atmosphere. A little known fact among Earthlings is that our ships run on a very simple and plentiful fuel: plain old water. Usually acquiring more, especially on a planet like Earth, is easy. On this night, however, we were on a farm in rural Canada, far from any lakes or rivers.

"There's a farmhouse a few hundred yards away," Khrelan observed. "They're bound to have water tanks or a well."

"Maybe we should just knock on the door and ask them for some," I joked.

"That's not a bad idea," Khrelan said. "Farm folks are usually nice people, right? They might be glad to help us. It's the neighborly thing to do. Besides, we could just wipe their memories afterwards, anyway."

The more I thought about it, the more I liked the idea. Wouldn't it be funny to just walk up to the house and ask for some water? Maybe I was just bored and looking for some excitement, but I needed an escape from the routine. In any case, I convinced Khrelan to join me. The commander was hesitant at first, but I was able to convince him that we could handle ourselves. Despite the incident with the man in the woods, we typically avoided revealing ourselves to humans, but it does happen in emergencies and sometimes by accident.

It was a chilly, overcast evening. The cold wind bit right through our uniforms as we walked across the field toward the farmhouse. The thrill and sheer absurdity of what we were doing made the walk quite enjoyable, though. It was also nice just to be out of the ship. We had our multi-tools with us and a container for the water. We only needed a few gallons to get our craft back to the mothership.

As we approached the house, we could see that the lights were on. The residents were apparently still awake. Khrelan got a little nervous at that point and said, "I don't know if we should do this. Let's look around the yard for a hose or faucet instead."

"Ah, don't be a Vyklax," I said. "Where's your sense of adventure?"

I was feeling good and having fun. I really didn't think there was anything to be afraid of. With a bounce in my step, I climbed the stairs to the front porch and walked right up to the door. I was about to knock when I decided instead to take a peek through the window to see what was going on in there. My timing was unfortunate. I put my hands up to block the glare and pressed my face to the glass only to see a woman's face right there, staring back at me! I shouted and jumped back, startled. She jumped, too, and started to scream.

"Jim! Jim!" I could hear her shouting. "There's one of them goddamn *aliens* out there!"

Then I heard Jim – her husband, I assumed – yelling from another part of the house: "What are you blathering about, woman? You been watching too many of those stupid movies again!"

"I swear!" the woman cried. "It was right there at the window! An ugly-ass, bug-eyed looking thing – just like the one the guy on the news reported!"

I knew she was referring to the man in the woods – the man we had tried to help.

I looked back at Khrelan, who was at the base of the porch steps, and shrugged. I didn't really know what to do. Well, I'll tell you, in a moment it became very clear what I needed to do. With no warning, the front door of the farmhouse flew open so forcefully that it almost came off its hinges. Standing in the open doorway was a huge bear of a man. He was wearing dirty overalls and clutching a shotgun. The sight of the massive hillbilly stunned me for a few seconds. All I could do was stare at the towering human. The man looked down at me in surprise and disgust.

"Jim? Do you see it?" the woman called from inside the house.

"I see it, Betty," Jim said, "and it is one *ugly* S.O.B."

Jim raised the shotgun and pointed it at my head. I froze in fear.

"Run!" Khrelan shouted. That caught Jim's attention and he swung the shotgun in Khrelan's direction.

"There's two of the bastards!" Jim yelled. "Maybe more! Stay inside, Betty. They might want to impregnate you."

"Oh, no!" Betty wailed. "Kill 'em, Jim!"

Jim had every intention of doing just that. He raised the shotgun to eye level and prepared to fire at Khrelan, who was now frozen in shock as I had been the moment before. I had a tiny window of opportunity. I knew I had to act! With reflexes I wasn't aware I even had, I quickly aimed my own weapon – the ever-versatile multi-tool – at Jim and zapped him with a stun beam. Jim was thrown back through the open door and landed on his back with a loud crash. Betty screamed. Khrelan started running. I stepped forward to get a look at Jim, who was lying prone and unconscious on the floor. He was still breathing. Betty had been standing in the front room during all of this. When she got a look at me, she instantly fainted.

Khrelan was long gone. I looked back to see him already halfway across the field. Even with those short little legs of his, he could sure fly when he was scared! I chuckled to myself. The whole scene was really rather humorous. I remembered then why we were there. Luckily, I still had the empty container. The interior of the house was silent. I was fairly certain there was no one else there, so I went into the kitchen and filled the container with water. On the way out of the house, I checked poor old Betty once more to make sure she would be okay. Jim, I knew, would wake up with a brutal headache, but he would live.

Mission accomplished, I walked casually back to the ship with the water. In all that excitement, I had adjusted to the cold and the walk felt pleasant. I chuckled out loud again when I visualized Khrelan running away from that farmhouse like a scared Ukaboro with its tails between its legs. I knew our farmhouse encounter would be a story we would laugh about for years to come. As for Jim and Betty, I can only imagine what they would tell their friends and family. They might even go to the media. They could probably make some money off of their story. Of course, they, like the majority of humans on this planet, have no idea what is really going on and why we are here. Someday, they'll understand. Until then, we'll be stationed here to keep an eye on things – which reminds me, I better get back to work.

Guardian

Who was he? Where did he come from? What happened to him? Starla pondered these questions each time she passed the filthy, disheveled figure huddled on the sidewalk near the entrance to the downtown office building in which she worked. The man looked broken, defeated, and miserable – totally alone amid the swarming masses. His clothes were tattered, his face caked with dirt. He reeked of sewage. He sat on a piece of cardboard with his eyes cast downward, a cup for handouts held in his grimy hand. Starla could not understand how someone had allowed his life to disintegrate so completely. Was it mental illness? Addiction? Trauma so profound that his mind simply could not recover? Whatever his reason, the homeless man had apparently given up on ever assimilating into the society that operated all around him, oblivious to his presence and unconcerned with his welfare.

      The homeless man fascinated Starla. She often thought about him on her way to work, wondering if he would be in his usual spot. Since his initial appearance, perhaps a month or so ago, he had consistently been there. A strange routine had developed – a relationship of sorts. The homeless man would keep his head down almost all the time, but when Starla would pass by, he would always look up, meet her gaze, and smile ever so slightly. At first it was creepy and Starla had difficulty returning the small social gesture, but as time passed, she had developed a soft spot for the man. While most pedestrians and passersby seemed to regard the homeless man as a mere object occupying valuable sidewalk space, an impediment to their progress down the street, Starla felt genuine sympathy for him – more than that – she felt true empathy for a fellow human being.

On a dreary, rainy morning in late September, Starla was riding the train to work. Her thoughts again returned to the homeless man. As she watched the rainfall quickly escalate into a torrential downpour, she wondered what it would be like to be stuck outside in such awful weather. Like an abandoned pet or a forgotten toy, she felt the loneliness must be crushing, the sorrow infinite. Starla watched the water droplets cascading down the window as her mind continue to wander.

When she got off the train, she opened an umbrella and began the short walk up the street that would take her to her building. The rain poured down from the ominous, gray sky. A few doors down from the office, Starla spotted the homeless man. As she had predicted, he was sitting in his usual spot and he was drenched. While the water bombarded him, he simply sat as usual, his hair matted and his clothes saturated, his cup held in an outstretched hand. Somehow, he seemed to sense Starla's approach. He lifted his head when she neared, looked her directly in the eye, and smiled. For the first time, Starla stopped when she reached him.

"You look cold," she said. "You should take this." Impulsively, Starla handed the umbrella to the soaked and shivering man.

He reached up and took it. An unusual expression appeared on his face – a thoughtful, serious look that made the man seem both wise and troubled. He nodded and said, "Are you sure you aren't going to need this?"

"I'll be fine," Starla replied. "I have another one."

"Thank you. Sincerely, thank you."

"No problem. Have a good day, okay?"

Starla continued toward the door to the building. As she reached for the handle, the homeless man spoke again.

"Hey," he called, "you work a lot. Have you ever considered taking a day off? It seems to me like you could use a vacation... like tomorrow, even."

Starla laughed. "I *wish*. This is the busiest time of year for us, and it only gets worse as we get closer to Christmas. I'd love to take time off, but I just can't."

"Please consider it. It might rain again tomorrow. Could be a perfect day to stay home and watch movies on the couch."

"That does sound lovely," Starla smiled. "I'll consider it."

Starla entered the building. The homeless man watched her go, the serious, concerned expression still etched on his face.

The day flew by. Starla worked hard as she always did. Her job required energy and focus, and when 5:30 rolled around, she was physically and mentally exhausted. She got on the elevator that would take her to the main floor lobby, eagerly anticipating her arrival at home. Her cat would be waiting for her. She visualized her beloved pet winding through her legs as she stepped through the door. It made her smile. She imagined pouring a glass of wine and enjoying a light meal in front of a good movie. She sighed out loud. *Soon*, she thought. When the elevator stopped, she stepped out, crossed the lobby, and exited the building.

Starla was lost in thought when she left the office. She was on autopilot as she started walking up the street to catch the train that would take her home. It had stopped raining, but she hardly noticed. Then a voice spoke, breaking the spell. It was the homeless man, seated on cardboard in his usual spot. "Rough day?" he asked.

"Oh, hello," Starla said. "It was a *long* day. My head is full of numbers and I just want to get home and relax."

"Gotcha. Well, remember what I said about taking a

day off. Call in sick tomorrow. Tell the boss you woke up
with a cold or something."

"Ha! It would take a lot more than that for me to
justify staying home. Nuke attack, maybe... or an alien
abduction..."

"An inter-dimensional wormhole localized to your
kitchen, which you accidentally stepped through and lost an
entire day?"

"That would work, yes."

"Good. Okay then, have a good night. Maybe I won't
see you tomorrow."

"Thanks. You too. See ya."

Starla continued on her way. She caught her train and
eventually arrived at home, where her cat was indeed
waiting. It purred and rubbed against her legs when she
entered the apartment. She reached down and ran a hand
down the cat's arching back before setting about doing
exactly what she had planned to do all afternoon. She
prepared a meal, poured a glass of wine, and collapsed on the
couch where she ate and imbibed, basking in the glow of the
flickering images on her television set. Before long, she
began to doze. She did not fight it. Sleep took her and she
was out until morning.

Starla awoke with the words of the homeless man
ringing in her head: *Take a day off. Call in sick.* She thought
about what lay ahead – another commute to the office,
another day of numbers, equations, and mind-numbing
statistics, another piece of her soul sacrificed to the machine
– and she seriously, if only briefly, considered taking the
man's advice. It would be wildly out of character for her, and
she concluded that she simply couldn't do it. She had built
her career on being reliable and responsible – an asset to her
company at all costs, including her own health, happiness,
and sanity. She went on with her morning routine and was

soon on her way out the door to catch the train.

It was a typically overcast morning. A thick fog hung in the air. A blanket of gloom stretched across the sky, blotting out the sun with its oppressive haze. Having spent her whole life in the large, coastal city, Starla was used to the weather, and knew that by noon the fog would dissipate and that clear blue would replace the dismal gray. Her instincts told her that it would not rain. Her intuition, quiet, yet persistent, spoke to her, too. It told her that something else was lurking in the atmosphere. She had a strange, lingering sense of foreboding as she walked briskly toward her stop to catch the train.

In usual fashion, the train arrived – each car tightly packed with passengers. When the door to the nearest car opened, Starla squeezed aboard, sliding herself between the tightly packed bodies. There was no window seat available for her this morning. She groaned and resigned herself to an uncomfortable, awkward ride downtown. Starla endured the bumpy, noisy, rumbling of the train as she was jostled and bumped by sweaty strangers.

As she rode, Starla escaped into a safe space deep in her mind, constructing an elaborate fantasy in which she walked barefoot on a deserted beach as the sun was setting. She could feel the cool breeze on her face and the sand between her toes. She could hear the roaring waves and the cries of seagulls. She could see the vast ocean, pounding waves, and the fiery orb of the sun sinking below the horizon. Starla's reverie was broken when the train suddenly lurched. Starla realized she was at her stop and pushed her way toward the door. She stepped off when it opened.

Upon her arrival in the city, Starla switched to full machine mode – a creature of routines, subroutines, thorough conditioning, and blunt programming. She merged with the other drones and marched up the street toward her office building. A self-absorbed man in an expensive suit with a cell phone pressed to his ear slammed his shoulder into hers as he stormed past, snapping Starla out of her fugue. "*Excuse* me!" Starla exclaimed as she spun to look back at the man who had so coldly barged past. The man did not stop to acknowledge her or apologize. Starla sighed and shook her head.

As she continued on her way, Starla heard something that immediately captured her attention – it was the sound of a child crying nearby. Alarmed, she looked around and tried to determine the source of the loud, pitiful sobs. No one else seemed at all concerned. The other pedestrians either did not hear or simply ignored the crying and went about their business. Starla could hear the wailing growing louder and more desperate. She realized it was coming from a narrow alley just ahead and moved forward quickly to investigate.

Peering into the dark, dank, trash-filled alley, Starla was shocked to see that the crying was indeed coming from a child – a boy of about five years of age. He was sitting on the ground with his back to a graffiti-covered wall, his head in his hands. He was sobbing uncontrollably. It was a wretched sight. Starla rushed to the child and knelt beside him. "Hey, there," she said gently. "Are you okay? Where are your mommy and daddy?"

The boy stopped crying, lifted his head, and looked Starla directly in the eyes. "*You're* my mommy... and I hate you. I want you to die. I want you to die right now."

Starla gasped. The boy's face had the look of pure malevolence, full of contempt and violence. Starla had the sudden sense that she was in the presence of something utterly evil and incredibly dangerous. She jumped to her feet and moved away from the boy. He stared at her, sneering, his eyes exuding malice.

"We've been waiting for you," the boy said as he

stood up.

Starla continued to back away in fear. The boy looked normal, but there was an inhuman glint in his eyes that disturbed Starla on a primal level. "What are you talking about?" she sputtered. "Who's been waiting for me?"

A figure appeared beside her – a tall man in a dark overcoat wearing a large hat that obscured the upper portion of his face. Starla shrieked. She had not seen the man approach. It was as if he had suddenly materialized from the shadows of the alley. The man raised a gaunt, bony hand and placed it on her trembling shoulder.

"Hello, Starla," he said in a deep, raspy voice. "It's nice to finally meet you. We've been waiting a very long time."

The grip on Starla's shoulder was abnormally firm. She tried to pull away but could not.

"What's going on?" she cried. "What do you want from me?"

"It's a little hard to explain, and – trust me – you really wouldn't understand even if I tried. What we want, though, is simple – we want your life."

Starla panicked. She writhed, screamed, and started to flail wildly, landing clumsy blows on the chest and face of the man. The man's grip was vice-like, however – the punches had no effect. Starla screamed louder: "Help! Help! Please, someone *help!!!*"

"Shut up," the boy said. "No one can hear you anyway. We've got a field up. Stop acting like a fool and let us do our job."

"Show some respect," the man admonished the boy. "Remember who she is, even if she doesn't."

"What are you talking about?" asked Starla. "Who *are* you people?"

"So many questions," the man replied. "Yet,

somewhere, buried deep in your heart, you know the answer to each of them. It's a shame what this war has done to our people... and yours. It hurts me to see a fellow warrior in such a sad state of ignorance. The veil of forgetfulness is so thick now that you, like all the other tragic souls on this planet, probably have no idea what is really going on."

"Just do it!" the boy shouted. "I hate this place and this stupid skin suit. Finish the job and let's go."

"In another time on another world, this woman was a better fighter than you and I ever will be," the man said. He raised his free hand, which now brandished a bizarre, mechanical implement that resembled a small cattle prod. It glowed blue and emitted electrical sparks as the man brought it up toward Starla's neck.

In a furious instant, Starla summoned her strength and spun out of the man's grip. She instinctively and expertly disarmed him with a swift and accurate kick. It connected with the man's wrist and sent the device flying. Starla swung at the man's face. A perfectly executed jab to the jaw sent him reeling. With a wild scream, she rushed at him. Something had been unlocked. A latent power had been released.

Starla, in the chaos of the moment, felt as if she had left her body and was simply observing herself as she fought. In a hidden, difficult to access part of her mind, recognition and remembrance stirred, offering faint glimpses into another reality, another life.

Her flight of nostalgia was short-lived. The present returned with a painful jolt. The boy had jumped onto her back and was choking her from behind. Starla tried to throw him off, but he clung like a rabid monkey. The man in the dark overcoat moved forward, again wielding the glowing weapon. Starla could feel her consciousness ebbing away as the boy squeezed harder. She was drifting... drifting... and then suddenly the weight on her back felt as though it had been ripped away. The arm around her throat released.

Starla choked, sputtered, and gulped air as she struggled to regain her breath. When her awareness fully returned, the first thing she saw was the man in the dark overcoat. His posture was tense and he was scowling at something or someone behind her. Starla spun around and there, before her, grappling with the boy, was the homeless man from up the street. He smiled and winked at her as their eyes met.

"You were doing fine," he said, "but I thought you could use just a little help."

"*You* – " the man in the coat sneered, "that awful costume can't hide your essence. I was just beginning to think that I wouldn't have to contend with *your* kind on this mission."

"Not me," groaned the boy from his subdued position on the ground. "I knew one of these assholes would show up. We should have finished the job quicker."

"It was a valiant effort," said the homeless man as he crouched with a knee planted in the small of the boy's back. With one arm, he secured the boy's wrists. With his free hand, the homeless man reached into his pocket and retrieved an item nearly identical to the strange device previously held by the man in the overcoat.

"Thanks for playing," the homeless man said. "Better luck next time."

He pressed the device to the boy's neck and the boy disintegrated instantly with a flash of light and an explosion of fine, luminous particles. Starla, who had been standing silently in shock since making eye contact with the homeless man, shrieked when she saw the boy vanish.

The homeless man got to his feet, brushed off the dust, and said, "Kids these days... they have no manners."

"This is all so crazy," Starla said. "Were you

following me?"

"Yes, but probably not for the reasons you might suspect. As you know now, I wasn't the only one following you, either."

"I don't understand."

"I know, but someday you will. You are a very special person with a very special role to play. That's all I can tell you right now."

The man in the overcoat sighed. "So, how shall we finish this? I don't know if I can handle another fight. Physical combat is so tedious and boring."

"You know what to do," replied the homeless man. "Or do you want me to do it for you?"

"Fair enough. I thought we had her this time. Well played. I'll see you again, I'm sure."

The man in the overcoat brought his weapon up and held it to his own neck. In a flash of light and dust, he disappeared, leaving an eerie cloud hanging in the air. Starla watched as it quickly dissipated. She did not cry out this time.

"Score one for the good guys," smiled the homeless man.

"I can't pretend that I have any idea what is going on here," Starla said, "but I know that I owe you my gratitude. Thank you."

"No, thank *you*," the homeless man said. "It's been an honor."

"What should I do now? What's going to happen to you?"

"Go to work. Get on with your normal life, however hard it might be. I have other duties to tend to, other places to go."

"Nothing will ever be normal again."

"Good. This universe is full of things that most

human beings will never be aware of. You've had a taste of the mystery. There will be more. For now, take what you have experienced and know that at any moment you may be called upon to participate in the bigger picture, the Grand Cosmic Design."

"I'll try. It may be difficult to relate to the so-called *real* world now, but I'll try."

"Don't try to relate. Be yourself."

"I better get going then. I don't want to be any later for work than I already am."

The homeless man smiled. "That's the spirit. Do what is right for you *now*. The path will open up when it is time. Life itself is an adventure. There is nothing mundane about existence."

Starla smiled back. "I like that. Thank you, again."

"Bye, Starla."

Starla left the alley. She merged with the other pedestrians and continued on her way to work. She looked around and, for the first time, she truly appreciated her surroundings. The sky, the sun, the street, the buildings – even the swarming masses of drone-like people, were all imbued with beauty and grandeur, all things part of the Grand Design. Starla wondered how many others were aware of what occurred behind the scenes, above their city and all around them. The small glimpse she had gotten of another reality, concurrent with her own, made her head reel and her heart race when she considered how much more existed beyond her perception. As she contemplated, she reached her office building. Before entering, she took one last look up at the bright, blue sky. *There are stars up there,* she thought. *I can't see them right now, but I know they're there.*

The Woods

My nightmare began as a simple walk in the woods. It had been a hard day and I just needed a little fresh air and exercise. I thought a short hike through the forest behind the office building would be the perfect remedy for the stress I had been feeling. I had no idea then that I would soon find myself lost and wandering through Hell.

To be clear, I don't *hate* my job. Let's just say that designing software is a lot less fun and creative – and a lot more tedious and frustrating – than I expected. I had been really struggling with a piece of code, ready to pull my hair out and put a fist through the monitor. Iteration after iteration, nothing worked. I was sweating, cursing, and near tears. Bobby, who works in the cubicle next to me, knew I was getting more and more upset. He poked his head over the wall and said, "You should take a walk, buddy. I can hear your frustration. Take a break before you totally lose it." It was good advice. I immediately thought of the trail that winds through the woods behind the building. I thanked Bobby for his wise suggestion and was out of my seat and out the door in a flash. I didn't even bother to back up my work.

It was late afternoon when I stepped outside. It was sunny, but not too hot, and there were big, fluffy clouds moving through the sky – it was a perfect day for a walk. I took a deep breath and walked around to the back of the building, already beginning to feel rejuvenated.

At the trailhead, I paused. I felt a subtle fear sweep over me, as if I stood before the open, gaping mouth of some hideous, ancient creature. The forest, in that moment, seemed to be alive in a way I hadn't noticed before. It was a vast, singular, mighty organism... and I was about to willfully walk right into its belly. I shook off the fear, convincing myself it was unfounded and foolish, and crossed the threshold.

As soon as I entered the woods, I became aware of a shift in the quality and volume of the sounds around me. It was like I had stepped through a portal into another dimension. I could hear birds, the rustling of leaves, twigs snapping beneath my shoes, and the unsettling scurry of small, unseen creatures. The sounds were sharper and more distinct than those I had perceived outside of the forest. My ears suddenly seemed to be much more sensitive, my hearing more acute. I stopped to listen more carefully, my brain finely tuned to the activity of the woods.

There occurred then a weird synesthesia – I began to actually *feel* the sounds. It was like music – amazing, otherworldly music, and it caused ripples of pleasure to roll up and down my arms and all over my body. My heart fluttered as if I had just jumped out of an airplane. My scalp tingled and a delicious, warm sensation enveloped me. It only lasted a minute or so, then it faded. I assumed that I was simply feeling the powerful healing and restorative effects that come from spending time in nature, which can be especially beneficial for someone like me who spends so much time indoors staring at a computer monitor. I did not suspect that anything unusual or extraordinary was happening. Boy, was I wrong.

Feeling great, I continued along the meandering trail. A few yards in, I stopped and turned around. I was shocked to see that I could no longer recognize the spot where I had entered the woods. The trees had closed in around me entirely. *Have I really hiked that far in?* I wondered. As far as I could tell, I had only been walking for a few minutes, but I had already lost sight of the trailhead and the edge of the forest. In fact, I could not even see the treeline. The foliage was so dense that even the light of the sun struggled to pierce the thick brush. It had grown considerably darker. I momentarily panicked in my disorientation until I realized that I had not stepped off the trail. I posited that if I were to turn around, the path would lead me straight back out of the woods. I assured myself that I had nothing to fear. Again, I was wrong.

As soon as I regained my composure, I saw it... If only I hadn't! I believe now that it wanted to be seen. Perhaps the awful thing had even drawn me to it. There it was, just off the trail, growing at the base of a tall pine. It was an obscene sight! At first I thought it was a dead animal, one that had met a violent demise – at first glance, it looked like a small creature that had been torn apart and turned inside out. It was the color, texture, and vague shape of organs and viscera. My mind recoiled at the hideous thing until I realized that what I was looking at was not an animal, but a plant of some sort – a peculiar pod with lobes, flaps, and tentacles. It was the color of flesh and it was clearly growing out of the ground.

As I stared at the repulsive pod and tried to understand exactly what in the world it was, it suddenly seemed to move. *That's just the wind*, I reasoned, but then it moved again. It did not sway – it *twitched.* I froze. It twitched again. In that moment, I should have run, as fast I could without looking back, but instead, I let curiosity get the better of me. Despite my growing unease, I foolishly stepped forward to get a better look at the vile thing growing in the woods. I leaned in and a horrible, repugnant stench assaulted me. The pod stunk worse than death. I covered my nose and mouth with my left hand and crouched down beside the bizarre specimen. I was utterly fascinated by it. It was unlike anything I had ever seen – a flora/fauna hybrid. It looked alien. My inquisitiveness compelled me to get an even closer look. Wanting to touch it, I reached out. Just as I was about to make contact, the pod suddenly sprung open. The last thing I recall seeing before I lost consciousness was a squirming tongue-like appendage inside the pod – it ejected a cloud of yellow dust directly in my face.

When I awoke, I was on my back. It was cold and dark. The sun had gone down. Overhead, the full moon, ominous and dispassionate, illuminated the forest with spectral shades of blue and white. I tried to sit up, but I could not. For a terrible moment, I was completely paralyzed, my body and limbs numb and unresponsive. My brain screamed: "Move! Get up! Run!" but my body remained prone and useless. I squelched the shrieking voice in my head, overriding it with an internal mantra of calming words: *Relax, breathe, focus...*

Through pure force of will, I commanded first my arms to move, ever so slightly, then my legs. I could feel my strength returning. I wiggled my toes and fingers. Soon, I was able to lift my hands. I used my forearms to pull myself up to my elbows. From there, I was able to assume a sitting position with my legs folded beneath me.

I felt dizzy, dazed, drugged. The memory of what had happened before I had lost consciousness returned to me, as did the fear, which was infused with a surge of strength. I was able to get to my feet and the first thing I did was spin around to get a look at the grotesque pod-plant that had blasted me with spores. I could not see it! I walked over to the spot where I had discovered it. I approached, slowly, cautiously, but it was not there. I could clearly see where it had been, though. The soil was disturbed and there was a small trench, but the *thing* had disappeared. Could it have walked away? *No,* I told myself. *That's impossible... isn't it?*

As it grew darker, I realized that I had more important issues to worry about than the pod-plant. Night was coming and I needed to find a way out of the forest. I wondered if my co-workers thought I had finally snapped and walked off the job for good. I wondered if I had put my employment in jeopardy.

My imagination started to act up: *What if I were truly lost? What if ended up wandering around the woods for days?* As a bachelor, no one waited for me at home. An extended absence would certainly cause concern among my family and friends, but how many days or weeks would it take before they realized I was missing? I dismissed these thoughts and reminded myself that I was in a small, wooded area close to work. It would be virtually impossible to get lost... plus, Bobby, my co-worker, knew that I had only gone for a walk. I just had to stay calm and find my way out.

My eyes were beginning to adjust to the darkness of the moon-lit woods. To my left, just off the trail, I could see the spot where I had encountered the strange and dangerous plant. It was now gone, but the memory of its ghastly appearance caused me to shudder. Still, knowing where it had been, I was able to orientate myself. I turned in the direction I recalled entering the woods and began to walk.

With renewed courage and the utmost certainty that I would soon find my way back to the comfort and familiarity of civilization – only yards beyond, but seemingly a universe away – I marched on, trying to ignore the spooky sounds around me. I could hear rustling, crunching, whispering in all directions, like an invisible band of wraiths trailing me. The eerie noises, coupled with the pale, bluish light of the moon, soon unnerved me once again. My heart raced and a cold sweat covered my flesh. I quickened my pace.

I scanned the thick, dark woods on either side of the trail, straining my eyes looking for any sign of danger – then I almost walked right into the jaws of the beast. I turned my head and there it was, directly in front of me, blocking the trail – a massive, white wolf with eyes that glowed blood-red. It was hunched and snarling, ropes of saliva dangling from its exposed fangs. It was a monstrous sight, but it was also impressive, beautiful, mesmerizing. I had never seen such an unusual creature, either in reality or in pictures. Its fur was a pure, untarnished shade of brilliant white and its eyes glowed in such an uncanny way that they appeared to be self-luminous... And its size! Even hunched over, ready to pounce, the beast was nearly as tall as me. It was more a mutant or a monster than a wolf.

Of course, I was terrified. It was a dizzying, nauseating, mortal fear that penetrated and filled the very core of my being. Time stood still. I looked into the eyes of the beast and saw the abyss, where I would soon reside, if it chose to attack. I slowly raised my hands in a show of submission and respect. "Whoa. Easy there, big guy," I said gently as I took a few steps back. Without warning, the beast lunged. I gasped as it bounded forward. When it was only a few feet away, the beast stopped suddenly and – here's where it gets truly bizarre – its lips curled into a subtle and very human smile. The wolf-beast, like something out of a surrealistic dream, sat on its haunches. It raised its snout to the moon and laughed manically. Yes, it *laughed.* It did not bark, it did not howl – it *laughed*, loud and heartily, as if it had enjoyed scaring the ever-loving shit out of me... which it had done.

I stopped and simply stared, my mouth agape, my mind struggling to comprehend what I was seeing. As I stood there watching like a dumbfounded imbecile, the great beast got up, fixed me once more with those intense, piercing, blood-red eyes, and shambled off the trail, vanishing into the woods. The trees swallowed the beast and it was gone, leaving no trace. I listened for any signs of its presence in the bush, but the forest was oddly silent. Even the normal ambient sounds seemed to have been muted. I had the feeling that I had just encountered something supernatural. I started to question my whereabouts. I started to question my sanity.

There was no time to waste. I did not have the luxury of pondering the structure of reality, my place in the cosmos, or the fragility of my psyche. It was the middle of the night and I was tired, hungry, and wandering through the forest. I needed to get out. I needed to get home. The trail in front of me was now clear. I chose to ignore the inexplicable nature of the events I had just experienced and soldiered on. I was hopeful that just up ahead was the trailhead – the place where I had entered the woods and unknowingly stepped into a nightmare.

Carefully, I crept up the trail, half expecting, half wishing, to see the bush open up in front of me to reveal the building in which I worked and deliver me to safety. This did not happen. I walked on for what felt like an hour. Was I going the wrong way? Could I have somehow gotten turned around? Was I plunging deeper into the heart of the forest? Panic again clawed at my brain, but I pushed it away with a few deep breaths. Suddenly, there it was! I could see the building beyond the treeline, silhouetted against the night sky.

Relief, sweet and ecstatic, poured over me like a shower from the heavens. I started to run toward the exit, ready to burst out into the glorious open space that awaited me on the other side. I was grinning like a fool and practically crying with joy as I bounded up the trail, but the smile on my face quickly melted away as I realized something most disturbing: I was not getting any closer to the black, rectangular shape of the office building looming ahead. Instead, it seemed to be receding into the distance as I ran. At first, my mind refused to acknowledge this startling fact – I kept running... but the building was moving *away* from me, as if being pulled by some powerful, mysterious force.

I stopped running. The building remained fixed in its position. I started jogging again, slowly at first, attentively observing the objects in front of me. I was making progress on the trail, getting closer and closer to the trees directly ahead, but to my dismay, the office building continued to recede into the distance! I refused to accept this spatial and optical anomaly and barreled forward, switching gears into a full-on sprint.

I was fast approaching the forest's edge. I could see the gap in the trees where I had entered so many hours ago. I summoned all of my strength and pushed toward it. Just as I was about to reach the threshold, the trees on either side of the opening suddenly came alive. In a coordinated maneuver, they moved as a singular entity, bending down and swinging into position. In an instant, the opening was blocked. The forest had sealed me in.

"No!" I cried as my energy and vitality drained away. My mind reeled in disbelief and my soul ached in defeat. I collapsed on the trail, withering into a sitting position with my head in my hands. I sobbed pitiful, wailing sobs as I grasped the hopelessness of my situation. Tears streamed down my face as I whimpered and mourned for the rational world I once inhabited.

In the vicious grip of despair, under the crushing weight of psychological anguish so enormous that I felt nearly suffocated by the hopelessness, I had a revelation. It struck at once with resounding force. In my hour of desperation, the truth was revealed to me – a savage and pure truth. The dawning of my understanding coincided with the dawning of a new day. I could see the faint glow of early morning through the gaps in the trees that now served as the bars of my prison.

I got to my feet and, as I rose, my strength returned and my will to survive increased with fresh intensity. My predicament started to make sense, at least in that moment. My mind had been thoroughly tested – expanded, even – by events of the rarest and strangest variety. I decided to confront what I perceived to be the source of my tribulation. In a small, timid voice that grew more powerful as I spoke, I addressed the forest itself:

"Hello, there. I think I am starting to understand what is happening. First, I would like to assure you that I mean no harm... although I'm sure that, even if I did, I would have very little power to do so."

The trees in my immediate vicinity swayed slightly, as if a gentle breeze had caressed them, though I did not feel it myself. I had the distinct sensation that my words were being heard. I continued: "It seems to me that I am the subject of – for lack of a better term – a *game*. Now, normally, I am not one to ruin someone's fun, but I am an unwilling – and until only moments ago, *unwitting* – participant, and *I'm* not having any fun at all. Is that the point? To torture and torment an innocent, ignorant, helpless individual? Is the goal to drive me insane? Do you get off on my suffering?"

The more I spoke, the angrier I became. Indignation filled my voice with courage and conviction. My words resonated through the woods. As if in response, a chorus of birds somewhere overhead erupted into song, the notes plaintive and sorrowful... and almost apologetic.

"I have had enough. I want to go home now. I want to be released."

Again, the trees around me swayed in a wave-like fashion that rippled through the bush. The birds had gone silent and, in the quiet interlude, something else caught my attention: a large, gray squirrel clinging to the trunk of a tree to my left. It was looking directly at me, its tiny, black eyes both wild and wise. It scampered down the tree and ran right up to me. It stopped at my feet and peered up.

"Hi, little buddy," I said.

The squirrel nodded its head and began to trot up the trail. A few feet away, it stopped and turned back to look at me. I realized then that it wanted me to follow it, so I did. I followed the squirrel for a hundred feet or so, until we came to the spot where the trees had closed in on the trail and sealed me in. The squirrel let out a funny little squeak and then ran off into the bush. Before me, the trees began to move. It was an astonishing thing to witness! As I watched, the trees bent back and returned to their original positions, opening the way for me to leave the woods.

Through the clearing I walked. I could see the office building where I worked getting bigger – closer. My thoughts drifted to the code I had been working on the day before – that frustrating little piece of information that I had so clumsily been trying to manipulate and conform to my desire. All around me – and within me, too – nature seemed to operate so effortlessly. Was there a hidden code behind it? Some special, secret algorithm that governed it all? My experience in the woods had made me feel like a toy at the mercy of a masterful programmer. I stepped out of the woods and into the light of a new day, with renewed appreciation for the complexity and beauty of the natural world.

Space Jelly Rides the Solar Wind

Picture now, a rare form of space jelly riding the solar wind. Visible inside its nebulous structure, strange activity is occurring – a chain reaction triggered at the atomic level, an electric dream. Colors appear and shapes writhe within the membrane. The jelly reacts – it is a response approaching emotion. Simultaneously, a man in bed on Earth stirs in a deep sleep. A connection is made and information is transferred. Astronauts in secret craft observe the jelly receiving the signal. They watch the holographic image projected by the unaware (dreaming) human into the unaware (non-sentient) jelly. They note the lifelike, three-dimensional quality of the image and perceive a most subtle transformation. The space jelly rides the solar wind and carries the man's dream into interstellar space.

The astronauts engage in mundane conversation. They are waiting for something. After a short time, some *thing* approaches from the nether regions of the system. The astronauts gather around the window of the craft and peer out into the inky abyss. More gelatinous matter from the heart of the galaxy now floats by, inside of which is suspended a moving image. The objects displayed in the jelly and their actions are clear and distinct, like an animated diorama encased within soft glass. The astronauts are excited.

"Follow this one," the mission commander says. "Observe! Study! Record!"

The craft begins trailing the jelly and the crew watch the action closely. They see a man seated at a desk hunched over a computer in a small, cluttered apartment. He is disheveled and apparently distraught. He is hammering away

furiously at the keyboard, his red, bulging eyes fixed on his
fingers as they fly across the keys. A bead of sweat forms on
his brow. It drops directly onto the 'B' key, unnoticed by the
raging typist. The scene transforms with a zoom-in on the
words forming on the monitor of the man's computer. The
astronauts are now able to read what the man is typing. The
frenzied writing exposes the unusual ideas and abstract
visions percolating within the man's brain. Characters race
across the screen and arrange themselves into words. The
words march forward and fall into place. Sentences
materialize. It is weird stuff:

> The central issue tonight is faulty
> equipment, flaws in thought that spiral out
> into a thing of unique beauty. We're gathering
> momentum together, you and I. Each man is a
> ripple in the fabric and the cause and result of
> every other man. It's a hive mind on this level,
> perhaps a writhing mass of stars on the next.

> In my world, we argue about origins
> and never get anywhere. It's a jungle, and the
> light breaking through the canopy is
> terrifying. I'm just telling you now what I feel,
> what I sense, what I perceive. What is truth?
> Who designed this maze? I wonder... and I am
> once again ensnared. In my short life, I have
> triggered every trap built into the structure of
> this reality.

> As a child, I practiced drawing the
> rings of Saturn. Around and around, over and
> over, on and on, a dance of circles, until
> something gave – a random mutation, a
> broken orbit, a new perspective – an

experience for the child who then makes a new connection and sends the particles on a fresh course. Energy is gained and ultimately released, discharged once again and recycled.

Now, it seems like choice has always been an illusion... or is that, too, part of my fantasy? How many others share my delusion? Where do *they* start their stories? I'm getting carried away. Typical.

I no longer need to keep looking for magic on the quantum or stellar scale – it's all right here in this tiny, cluttered room. It's here *right now*, vibrating through my fingers and into the dirty plastic keys. Somehow, I am able to summon it, momentarily hold it in the air before me – pure, foolish electricity gathered from the void! I see it! The circuit holds, the flow is maintained... and then it begins to waver. Confidence falters and the grip is released. Did I trigger another trap?

In the end, it won't matter if every single word is swallowed by the black hole. The world is changing. The universe is constantly transforming. Will we all disappear into the machine and provide the Big Mind with new forms? I've been so desperate to leave something of substance behind, to create, to define myself by my work or craft or ideas, to justify my existence... but I'm lazy, sloppy – betrayed at the chemical level. Is it low self-esteem or total awareness of – and profound respect for – life's potential? Are human beings simply conduits, receptors, receivers, gathering energy and reorganizing it? The questions come in waves through some sort of valve function or inhibitor. There is a rhythmic response.

If human beings are information nodes – high-density idea-gathering points (the data processing systems of the universe), then this writing isn't such a filthy activity after all. In my mind, the concept is enormous and I am humbled when I see my goofy attempts at articulation manifest something. It's not much, but it's *something...*

The astronauts in their secret craft are thoroughly engrossed. The writer has opened up a window to his soul. The observers peer directly in. The scientific value of what they are seeing is not clear, but they continue to study it anyway, in the spirit of pure research. The man at the keyboard is still typing away like a madman, attacking the keys with spastic, flailing fingers, carving his thoughts onto the page:

I've convinced myself that this is combat journalism and that I am exhibiting courage under fire. What a terrible idea – a bad thought that could grow to consume me. Still, what a simple solution! Here on the page, it happens instantly, in this moment, my moment now, your moment forever.

Ah, but the writing is becoming erratic. I am losing the plot. My grip on the reigns of thought is slipping. Abstraction and mental masturbation are taking over.

God, the time is too long. I could not
resist that one song. I could not sit still when
the music played. The son of the universe
under the lights. The son of his mother under
the lights, dead men in his head.

The music – glass in a dream, a
missing tooth. When I was young, I
contemplated eternity and drew pictures.
When I grew spirit hands, I held blood on
blood. Two colors, two ways to face the sun.
There is no mystery in this. There is no
mystery in my sleep. There is no history in
this song. There is magic in all songs.

It came to me again this morning, with
a headache and some regret: you are what you
don't excrete. I'm still a slave to that memory,
and as the birds sing in their vast prisons, I
choke on the notes. Now that the sun is up and
I can't lie to myself anymore, what are my
options? I feel far from the Source... or maybe
just torn on the inside, an emotional thing,
unrelated to the essence – like writing about
music or singing the truth. Split apart – I am
two... and three when the words work. I'm
choosing the words carefully tonight, charged
by the Big Mind and its satellite. Sigil magic,
some would say.

What I've done is convinced myself
that using language to participate in the battle
will allow me to play some sort of impossible
spectator role. I seem to be trying to display
my struggle in such a way that its wonderful
significance will be glaringly, brilliantly

apparent... but, nope – it's mundane and my painting is primitive and obvious. Self-sabotage, auto-examination, hardcore déjà vu. I'm writing a song that no one will hear.

I went for a walk and a bird followed me home. It was fun. You forget how playful nature is when you sit in a room for too long. You forget a lot of things. The room and the mind become one. My room is not only filthy and cluttered, but there are rat-people scurrying around in the walls and sounds that creep in through the cracks. There are real people out there – I know this – but they take on phantom forms. My neighbors become a manifestation of my guilt. Twisted, angry faces, friends who now hate me, shadow creatures feeding on my pain – is this a nightmare? If I tap away like this long enough, I bet a little truth will be revealed, a little skin exposed. They eat the skin, of course. Combat journalism!

The astronauts exchange worried glances. They are growing concerned for the man in the room who is pouring his wounded heart out onto the page as they watch in real-time. In the name of science, however, their study must continue. They are forbidden from interfering with the subject in any manner. They are simply there to observe and record their findings, even if it means having to watch passively as a mind completely unravels before their eyes. This would not be the first time.

The astronauts continue to watch as the man in the room stands up and begins pacing in small circles. He rubs his eyes with the palm of his hands. He scratches his unwashed, itchy head vigorously. He performs a sudden series of untrained, awkward karate kicks at an invisible opponent. With an enormous sigh, the man sits down at the computer. There is more that he wishes to express. After a few weird hand stretches and finger exercises, he leans in and begins typing again:

> This process used to scare the shit out of me. Still does, but not as much. It took a long time before I felt comfortable with myself and confident enough to write. Maybe I needed to suffer more before I had any right to work with words. I think a made a secret pact somewhere along the line, maybe before I was born, before the Earth gave form to this ridiculous collection of cells that became me. It may have been in a dream.

> There's a small, strong group of us – indignantly, defiantly wounded, eternally paying for the sins of our parents – on functioning terms with the shadow lurkers. Despite the chaos in our brains, we desire only peace. We are the children of hippies, for whom peace was a fantasy, a game, a fashion statement – but we have learned how to adapt. Nature always gets it right in the end.

> Here and there, nodes appear, powered by the collective mind, conjured by the guilt and horror of the herd – sunken aspects of the fabric, some strange movement of the tapestry itself. Ideas burst into being and scream for recognition, ready to conquer the entire thing

or die quietly in the corner.

There is a human being behind these words.

Some of us are truly and honestly challenged by the environment – forced into a flight-or-fight response – simply because we were born with something strong and abnormal. We are ready to take a stand for any convincing story that moves the soul! Ready to dance or die if that's what the moment calls for! Some were born to laugh at us. Fair enough.

In that moment, when the wood and metal meet the flesh, and the soul of the man becomes poetry – there, truth is born, the music is alive, brought forth from the primordial deep. It is a rendezvous at the center of the cross, where pre-time entities are conjured by some pitiful display of emotion. In my shame, they find sustenance... yet their feeding frees me from that burden I cannot name – that weight that makes the meat heavy.

Beauty comes like a conqueror to laugh at death and destroy every lost fragment still unconvinced. Will I be redeemed or annihilated? For now I am still flailing, still clinging to life, still dancing like an idiot to every random rhythm that moves me. Are you here with me now, phantom partner, drunk on my blood, farming my pain?

The man in the room abruptly stands up and steps

away from the computer. It is as if something has suddenly frightened him. Keeping his distance from the machine on the desk, as if it were a coiled rattlesnake about to strike, he begins pacing again, only this time in larger circles with his eyes locked on the monitor. He is now muttering to himself.

He freezes. Instantly, he is motionless and silent. Is he gathering his nerve for another dive into the fray? Is he steeling himself for another headlong rush into battle? Yes. Nostrils flare and an eye twitches... then, he is in motion. The man charges the desk and seats himself. The tempest of typing resumes:

> Experience, moment to moment without context, is meaningless. In music, each note anticipates the next. Here, in this realm, each phrase anticipates the next – and so it is in the greater reality. Life unfolds in a series of sensations and events, each seemingly isolated, but a larger perspective reveals the interconnectedness of all things. From the alpha to the omega, each component is part of the whole and also whole in itself – holographic, time in a bottle.

> The mind is a needle on a record, guided by the shape and texture of the material. It is trapped within the framework, bound by the architecture, and defined by the movement. The movement, it seems to me now, appears as chaos against a background of order – ripples of activity upon the surface of a perfectly smooth, balanced, and infinite expanse. Moreover, the mind is the fabric as well as the thread, the water and the waves.

The frantic writing ceases. The man at the desk exhales and his body relaxes. He sits back in his chair, his neck loose, his head rolling. He has been released from the throes of his maniacal creative frenzy and he is satisfied and spent. He basks in the pleasant afterglow, giving no thought to whether or not his words will ever be read.

Far above, on the outer fringe of the solar system, the astronauts in their secret craft also exhale and relax into their seats. They chatter quietly among themselves. They too seem satisfied. It has been an informative – and entertaining – viewing session.

"This is why I love this job!" exclaims one of the astronauts.

"Disengage," the mission commander says.

Boosters fire and the ship changes course, moving now away from the jelly and the projected thoughts of the writer in the room. The jelly carries the man's words into interstellar space.

Paradigm Shift

There are moments in life that are so significant, so momentous, that they completely alter one's perspective on the world. These moments serve as demarcation points, effectively separating the life of the individual into two distinct parts – life before the event and life after. Today, I experienced such an event and, though it has only been a few hours since the occurrence, it is already clear to me that from this day forward, my life will never be the same. Paradigm shift, reality upheaval, worldview or belief system reassessment – call it what you will – I have been changed. It's a story worth telling, so I am going to do just that. Bear with me. It's going to be a weird and wild ride.

I had classes this morning, just like I do every Monday. I'm in my second year at the university and my course load is heavy. The first unusual thing that happened to me today was that I woke up much earlier than I normally do. It was still dark out and my alarm wasn't set to go off for a few hours. I tried to get back to sleep, but I was already wide awake. I tossed and turned for a while before deciding to just get out of bed. My roommate was still fast asleep. I think he was out late last night partying, so, no real surprise there. I could hear him snoring away as I went down the hall of our apartment to the kitchen. I put on some coffee and sat at the table.

The nice thing about where we live is that we have a great view. The apartment building is on a hill and we are on the top floor. From our kitchen, we can see the school and most of the sprawling campus, which sits on a lake. It's actually quite scenic.

When the coffee was ready, I poured a cup and sat gazing out the window. The sun had just begun to come up. I was admiring the sight when I noticed something – a bright light slowly descending from the sky directly above the auditorium. It was clearly visible, a bluish-white point of illumination flashing in a strobe-like manner. It was interesting, but the sunrise was so beautiful – a magnificent display of deep reds and oranges, that I didn't pay too much attention to the falling light. Considering what happened later in the day and what I know now, I should have. The light seemed to disappear behind the building and I forgot about it.

I still had time to kill before my first class and, to be honest, I didn't want to be around when my roommate woke up and starting babbling about the crazy things he and his drunken frat boy friends had done the night before, so I gathered my stuff and left. I thought it would be a good opportunity to do some studying in the library. By the time I got outside, the sun was up. I felt good – it was nice to get an early start. The streets were quiet as I walked toward campus. It was serene and peaceful being out before most of the city had woken up. I had no idea then this day would be the strangest I had ever experienced.

When I got to the campus, I headed directly to the library. There were still very few people around, but I did notice a procession of vehicles moving toward the administration building – a line of black sedans with blacked-out windows. Again, I really didn't think much about it and just continued on my way. My mind was on a paper I've been working on. I was composing sentences and arranging paragraphs in my head. Who knew then that the writing I would end up doing today would be so much more interesting than that sterile academic stuff! Right now, my fingers are having a hard time even keeping up with the flow of thoughts. I must try to get this down before I forget the details.

Once I got to the library, I went to my favorite spot – an isolated desk by a window at the very back of the building. I pulled out my reference material and notebook and started into it. For some reason, it was a struggle. I could not seem to express what I was trying to say. Everything I tried failed. My ideas would not coalesce, the words would not work. Perplexed by my lack of productivity, I became frustrated. I knew that I needed to clear my head, so I decided to stretch my legs. Sometimes it helps if I step away from what I am doing and then return to it with a fresh perspective.

My plan was to go for a walk along the lake, but when I got outside, a sign posted by the entrance to the library caught my attention. I hadn't noticed it before. The sign announced the appearance of a guest speaker that very morning in the auditorium. The name and face of the speaker were very familiar to me, but it took a few moments before I remembered where I had heard of the individual. Then it came to me – the man was a researcher and speaker on some really out-there topics, like UFOs, aliens, government cover-ups, and other strange conspiracies. I had heard of the guy on the internet but had never really paid much attention to what he had said – or what he was selling. I'm a pretty skeptical guy when it comes to stuff like that. The sign said he was on a special tour of universities and that he had new and exciting information to share. I assumed it was a new book he was pushing, but for some reason, I was still curious. According to the sign, the talk was about to start. My paper was giving me grief and I still had time before class, so I thought, why not check it out? At the very least it could be good for a laugh, right? I'll tell you – I'm not laughing now.

For an early morning presentation, there were a surprising number of students gathered in the auditorium when I arrived. I'm not sure how many of them were there to hear the speaker and how many were there just to hang out, but there had to be over a hundred people in the room. As I recall, the man who was scheduled to present has a large online presence and a fairly loyal following of conspiracy geeks and UFO fanatics, but I was surprised to see so many people in attendance. I don't know how many true-believers there were, but I'm sure certain members of the audience – me included – were there simply out of curiosity... or for some laughs.

On the floor of the auditorium there was a small stage with a podium and a microphone. A large screen had been erected on the wall behind the stage. The stage was empty and the screen was blank. There was some quiet murmuring in the audience, but most of the students had their heads down and their eyes firmly planted on their phones and tablets. For some reason, I was drawn to an empty seat in the front row directly in front of the stage. Looking back now, I realize how out of character that was for me. I generally like to sit near the back when I attend a speech or lecture, but this time, I sat front and center. Perhaps I just didn't want to sit among the other students. The truth is, I have a hard time relating to most of them. Perhaps, on the other hand, I was guided by intuition or some other mysterious force. Well, for whatever reason, I sat at the front only ten feet or so from the stage.

I was in my seat for only a few minutes before the speaker entered the auditorium. He walked onto the stage and approached the podium. There was a small smattering of applause, but most people did not acknowledge his entrance or even look up from their devices. The lackluster welcoming did not faze the speaker. He carried himself with a confident swagger and had an intense, serious expression on his face. He immediately began to speak.

"Hello," he said. "Thank you for joining me this

morning. I think you will find this presentation informative and enlightening." The speaker pushed a button on a remote control that had been sitting on the podium. An image appeared on the screen behind him. It was an old and rather famous black and white photograph of a UFO – or flying saucer, as they were called in the days when the photo was taken. It's an image I had seen before and was intrigued by, despite my skepticism. The resolution and detail were quite impressive for a picture nearly 60 years old.

"I'm sure many of you have seen this photograph," the speaker said. "It is one of the earliest pictures of a UFO. It has been the subject of debate for decades. The object shown in this image resembles no known aircraft, then or now. It was taken by a respected and trusted senior member of the Air Force. It is not a hoax. It is a real picture of a real craft."

The speaker used the remote control to switch the picture on the screen to that of another famous shot of a UFO. This photograph was a full-color close-up of a flying disk over a field. It was one I had not seen. The clarity of the image was astounding. "This is not a hoax, either," the speaker said. "It looks too good to be true, but it's real. As is this..."

The speaker began cycling through photographs, each more convincing than the last. "And this. And this. These are actual pictures of unknown flying objects – unknown to the general public, at least. There are those in positions of power who have always known exactly what these things are... but more on that later."

The speaker now had my full attention. He had a commanding, convincing presence and the material was entertaining and totally fascinating. I looked around and was dismayed to see that most of the other students were disengaged. The majority of them were still fiddling with their phones or tablets. Some of the students were taking 'selfies' – obsessively, it seemed – one after the other. Between each shot they would check the result and then pose again, puckering their lips in a ridiculous and totally unattractive pout and making small adjustments to the angle of their head. I even noticed a few people yawning. Their loss, I thought.

The speaker used the remote control to dash through a long series of photographs of UFOs in rapid fire. Not all of them were disks. He showed pictures of ships that looked like luminous spheres, large cylinders, massive black triangles, and some that were shaped like acorns or bells. So many pictures at such a fast rate – I could not process them all. The speaker suddenly stopped his machine gun slide show and froze on an unsettling image. I recognized it instantly as the face and upper torso of a so-called 'Grey' alien, immediately identifiable and incredibly realistic. Was it a photo or CGI image? I couldn't tell. The bulbous head, large, black, insectoid eyes, tiny nose, and slit-like mouth of the creature were shown in life-like detail.

"I'm sure most of you are familiar with this little fella," the speaker said, "a typical, garden-variety Grey alien. We've all been conditioned to accept that this is what an extraterrestrial looks like. When we think of an alien, we think of this. I am here to tell you that we have been lied to. This little guy is nothing more than a standard psy-op, a diversionary tactic to steer you away from the truth. Would you like to know the truth?"

The speaker paused, waiting for a response. Aside from a few murmurs and shrugs, he was largely ignored. Those who weren't locked on their cell phones simply looked at him blankly. Impulsively and sympathetically, I answered him. "Yeah," I said, "I would like to know the truth."

The speaker heard me. He looked me in the eyes,

smiled, and said, "Good. That's what I like to hear."

I'm not sure why I spoke up like that. I think I just wanted the presenter to know that *someone* was following his talk and was interested in what he had to say. I'm still surprised that more people weren't curious. It was fascinating stuff! The speaker continued, unaffected by the ambivalence of his young audience.

"I am here today to make an announcement," the speaker said. "This lecture tour is for purely educational purposes and has nothing to do with selling a new book or video. I am not here to obfuscate the truth of the UFO and alien phenomenon by adding yet another theory or angle to the bloated subject. I have been tasked with a simple assignment – to disclose the facts. What I am about to reveal has been known to a select few for a very long time but, due to the sensitive nature of the material, it has been kept secret. Those in power believed people simply weren't ready to receive this information. Political, psychological, and religious factors made disclosure a dangerous prospect. However, the cultural climate of the world has changed and it has been decided that the general population is now ready for the truth."

Talk about an effective set up! I was totally riveted. I glanced around again and was shocked to see that most of the other students were *still* completely preoccupied with their gadgets. Such a self-absorbed, vain, narcissistic, narrow-minded group... Sometimes I fear for my generation.

"The truth is simple," said the man at the podium. "Aliens are real." The speaker paused, waiting for a response from the crowd. A few people shuffled in their seats. There was scattered murmuring and a cough or two. Someone behind me yawned loudly. Overall, the audience barely reacted.

"Yes, aliens are real and they have been with us for a

long time. They have, in fact, always been with us. But this," The speaker gestured toward the image of the Grey alien on the screen behind him, "is not what they look like. Here is a photograph of a real alien." The speaker pushed a button on the remote and the picture of the Grey was replaced by that of another humanoid entity, equally as bizarre.

The creature on the screen looked like a cross between a catfish and a man. It had two very expressive, very human, eyes. To me, they conveyed kindness, intelligence, and even a touch of playfulness. I was startled by the personality and character expressed in those eyes. The creature had a nose, but it was small and vaguely feline. The bottom portion of its face was the most unusual feature. Its mouth was large and fish-like and, despite the lack of lips, it seemed to be gently smiling. Stringy tendrils of skin dangled from its jaw like the whiskers of a catfish. The creature's skin was a very light shade of green, with hints of pink. It had long, flowing, silvery hair that obscured the creature's ears. I stared at the vivid and detailed image. Was it real? Was this another elaborate ruse? My mind recoiled and struggled to grasp what the speaker had just said and what I was now seeing.

"This particular individual," the speaker said, "is a good friend of mine. He enjoys blues music, long walks in the woods, Italian food, the occasional glass of red wine, and has a wickedly dry sense of humor. He is very obviously not human, but here's another secret – he is not from another planet. He and his kind are Earthlings, just like you and me. They have lived alongside our race since the dawn of time. We must accept the fact that we share this planet with other intelligent beings."

"What a load of shit," I heard a dude in a Greek-lettered shirt say.

"This is so, like, *dumb*," a gum-chewing girl in a too-tight sweater said.

"That thing is fuckin' *ugly!*" shouted some guy near the back. A burst of laughter from the mob followed. At this point, people began to leave the auditorium. I guess it was too much for most of them to accept... or maybe they were just bored. I stayed in my seat, eager to hear more. I wasn't totally convinced of the veracity of the presenter's claims, but I couldn't dismiss them entirely.

The man at the podium calmly watched as a large portion of the audience cleared out. He waited for the commotion to subside before speaking again: "To those of you who have chosen to remain, thank you. I am well aware that this is bizarre material. All I ask is that you keep an open mind and consider what I am revealing to you as a *possibility.* Think and decide for yourself."

While the man spoke, I found myself staring at the image of the creature on the screen, wondering what it would be like to actually meet it... or *him*, or whatever. I studied its features and allowed my imagination to wander. Would I be scared in its presence? Would I be in awe? Would it be possible to have a conversation? What would we discuss? The more I pondered it and the more I visualized an actual encounter, the more real it became for me.

At this point, I snapped out of my reverie. The presenter was now speaking about the long history of interactivity between the catfish creature's race and our own. He gave some compelling examples of their presence and the influences of their race, going all the way back to prehistory. According to the speaker, they had contributed in profound ways to nearly every aspect of civilization, even though the vast majority of people have been – and will remain – totally unaware of their existence. The man at the podium then said something that gave me the creeps: "Some of you have encountered these entities and were totally unaware. There may be some here on this campus right now."

That statement struck a nerve. A very strange sensation came over me – a sudden feeling of intense psychological distress. I'm not sure what happened, but it was as if the speaker's words had unlocked something buried in my subconscious – a hidden subroutine, a concealed sensory mechanism. My body broke out in a cold sweat and I began to tremble. My breathing became erratic and shallow. My head tingled and a weird pressure built in my skull, making my eyes throb. I inhaled and exhaled slowly, deeply, in an attempt to avert an imminent panic attack. I was successful.

I looked up to see the speaker scanning those who had remained in their seats with an amused sparkle in his eye. "Yes," he said, "there may, in fact, be such entities in this very room."

The words prompted me to turn to look at the people around me. I was alone in the front row. My eyes passed over the empty seats to my left as my neck slowly swiveled. There was a young woman sitting behind me a few rows back. Sitting in the seat next to her, as obvious as could be, was one of the catfish-men. The creature was dressed in contemporary and fashionable men's attire. It sat in a relaxed and confident posture, as if it didn't have a care in the world. The woman in the adjacent seat seemed to be entirely unaware of its presence. The creature returned my gaze and smiled. Skin tendrils dangling from its cheeks twitched.

For many moments, I could only stare. Had the creature been there the entire time? Why hadn't I noticed it before? The bizarre entity grew tired of my ogling. It made a frustrated gesture with its hands, shook its head, and looked away. The actuality of what I was perceiving was beginning to sink in. I looked around at the other people still gathered in the auditorium and was not surprised to see more of the catfish humanoids seated among them. There were just as many of *them*, it seemed, as us. I also realized then that I was not the only human who had begun seeing the creatures. There were a few other equally astounded students looking around the room. Like me, they seemed to be more amazed than frightened at the seemingly instant manifestation of the entities. Some people, I noticed, still had utterly blank expressions on their faces as they continued mindlessly playing with their hand-held gadgets.

"A small minority of you, I suspect, are beginning to understand," the man at the podium said. "The world you thought you inhabited is largely an illusion. There are many aspects of reality that are beyond the scope and grasp of what you have been conditioned to believe. I represent a group of people who feel that the human race is now ready to accept certain truths that were once too much for our immature species to handle. It may take time to adjust to the new reality... and some never will, unfortunately. For those who do, the future will be a very exciting time indeed. Our two races still have much to learn from each other."

I sat in stunned silence as the speaker concluded his lecture. When he was finished, enlivened chatter filled the auditorium. Students – human and catfish-kind alike – rose from their seats. Those who were unaware of what was happening around them filed out of the auditorium, somehow managing to walk while keeping their eyes fixed on their mobile devices. Those of us who could now see the entities among us lingered near our seats, unsure of how to proceed with our day-to-day existences. Finally, after an awkward minute of uncertainty and apprehension, I decided to act. I approached the nearest creature, held out my hand, and introduced myself.

www.ingramcontent.com/pod-product-compliance
Lightning Source LLC
Chambersburg PA
CBHW060140130626
46556CB00006B/2434